I0683310

Anansi Island

Anansi Island

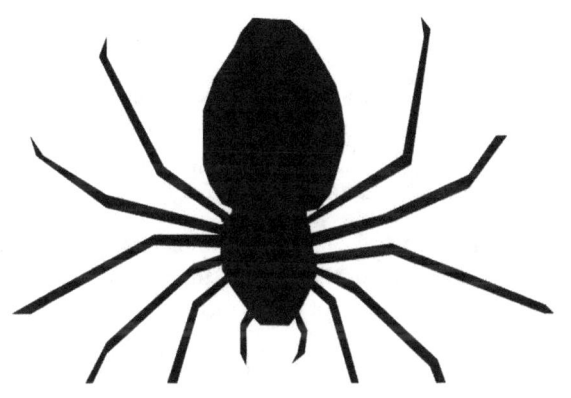

Nikki Bennett

To my Uncle Jimmy

The Island Chronicles Volume 2
Anansi Island
Text copyright © 2018 by Nicole A. Bennett
All rights reserved.
Cover art copyright ©2018 by Nicole a. Bennett
Published by Firedrake Books, LLC

ISBN-13: 978-1-941036-28-0

No part of this publication may be reproduced, or stored in a retrieval system, or transmitted in any form or by any other means, electronic, mechanical, photocopying, recording, or otherwise, without written permission of the publisher.

This book is a work of fiction. Characters, names, places and incidents are products of the author's imagination or are used in a fictitious manner and are not to be constructed as real.

Printed in the United States of America

Contents

AT SEA

This is a dream.

In this dream, a lonely island bobs in a vast orange sea. A mountain rises in the island's center, stark and gray and surrounded by a tangled jungle that creeps to the shore. Long white insects slither along the beach, waving dozens of red legs and snapping, poisonous pincers as they search for food. Giant centipedes. Mukade.

The mukade raise their heads to the sky. They detect, rather than see, an ominous black cloud engulfing the mountain. A living cloud, made up of hundreds of tiny black things.

Those things swarm the island, devouring everything. They eat the terrified mukade. The jungle. Every grass blade, every tree leaf, every slug.

Everything.

They even attack the people running out of a dark cave and screaming for help. The creatures cover the terrified kids, and when the swarm flies away, it leaves nothing except bones.

I jerk awake, sweat dripping into my eyes.

A dream.

I raise my head and try to refocus my terrified eyes. The orange sea ripples in front of me, stretching out to meet a

1

dense magenta sky. That horrible island has long since vanished beyond the horizon.

We escaped. We escaped right before the black things devoured everything.

I sit up, wide-awake. Next to me lies Steffi, her red hair splayed across the raft, her blue eyes shut tight in a restless sleep. Is she dreaming of the island too? Probably. We left two days ago. Only two days since Little Mike crumpled on the shore, overpowered by the black things. Since The Others frantically swam out to sea in an attempt to escape. Since eight of us, the lucky ones, floated away on a makeshift boat, leaving the others behind.

We didn't return for them. We left them to a horrible fate.

The little raft I'm sitting on is tied to the boat. Made of wood, tediously burned into a canoeish-type floating device, it holds four others. Malika's tight black curls poke above the edge. Keiko's long silky hair spills over the side. Rob sits next to Keiko; his brown hair ruffling in the breeze. Bhasker must be in the canoe too, because Steve and Sarah lie on the opposite raft. They're the largest, and their combined size fills most of the raft's free space. Steve's left arm trails in the warm seawater.

Eight of us. We survived the island and escaped a prison where we had once been doomed to spend the rest of our meager lives. Why we had been sentenced to this prison is anyone's guess.

Who had sentenced us is also a mystery.

Steffi thinks aliens sent us to this place. I'm not totally convinced. But I'll agree that we aren't on Earth. This world is too crazy different from ours. For one thing, the orange sea is poisonous if you haven't developed an immunity to it. And the vibrant sky doesn't have a sun or moon or stars. During the day, the sky glows so we can see, but when night comes, it comes in an abrupt jolt. One minute the world is light, the next it's pitch black.

Then there's my pet bat, Spike. He's another weird prod-uct of this world. In this place, bats can tell you secrets to help you survive, *if* you can understand what they say. Most people can't. Out of us eight, I'm the one Spike communicates with.

Steffi rolls over and yawns. Her blue eyes open and stare at the sky. "What time is it?"

"Day time," I say.

"Where are we?"

"In the middle of the sea, Steffi. Just like yesterday."

Spike the bat flits over to me and chirps. He's only a few months old and talks in a baby bat garble. I understood the adult bats, back on Mukade Island, but I have a hard time fig-uring out Spike's chatter.

He's trying to tell me something now, but I can't quite understand him.

Steffi sits up and stretches. "Is land any closer?"

"Not sure, but I know how to find out."

My naked eye can't spot land, but the strange brass tele-scope we found buried on Mukade Island will show me any-thing I want to see, no matter how far away it is.

"Hey Rob!" I yell.

Rob's sleepy eyes peek over the canoe's side. "What?"

"Pass me the telescope, would you?"

He digs through the canoe, finds the telescope, and shim-mies out across the boat's outrigger towards me. He stops to yawn, slips, and splashes into the orange water.

Steffi laughs. I grab the telescope before Rob drops it. He clings to the other end, spluttering.

"How's the water this morning?" Steffi says.

"Cold." Rob lets the telescope go and swims from under the outriggers, drinking the seawater as he strokes. The seawater is like a five-course meal when we drink it. It also cleans us when we're dirty. We've already gotten into the habit of swim-ming beside the rafts for a few hours a day. The canoe and

3

its rafts are horribly cramped with eight of us, plus swimming helps our limbs stay supple.

I peer through the telescope as Rob splashes around the raft. The shapes are blurry but soon come into focus. A flat island with a small bump, a tiny hill maybe, comes into view. But I see even more.

The crazy thing about this telescope is, the harder you stare into the end, the more you can zoom up on things. I stare into it, and the island looms closer. Pretty soon I can focus on grains of sand on the beach.

Kids live on this island. I've seen them before, but they aren't up yet. I don't see any mukade, but they avoid the light. They've probably scooted back to their lair for the day.

"We're closer," I tell Steffi, "and we're still on course. I'd say we have a couple days out here on this sea before we reach that island, though."

Steffi sighs. "Bleh."

I search the horizon. The island we escaped, Mukade Island, lies behind us. I keep waiting for the cloud of black things to pass over us and head for the island we're trying to reach. But I see no sign of it. The *things* must have gone back the way they came, their hunger satiated for now.

Immersing yourself in the seawater is the only way to avoid the black things. That part is tricky because the seawater is poison to most people. It burns them if they touch it. But the eight of us are immune. We became immune in a weird way: we got bit by mukade. Instead of killing us, their venom spread through our veins and a weird change happened in our bodies. The same seawater that used to burn us became our life source. It helped us grow strong.

The water also cures old injuries. Steve, the oldest of us, used to have a dead eye. He would cover the red and unseeing orb with a patch, but after a few weeks swimming in the sea his eye returned to normal.

4

I zoom in on the island we left. "There's Mukade Island," I say.

"See anything moving on it?" Steffi asks.

Tall black trees surround the glade where we built our canoe. The trees still stand although most of their leaves are gone. The black things ate those.

"I see three kids on the beach," I say.

"So some of 'em survived," Steffi murmurs. She has a relieved look on her face. Maybe she's feeling guilty for leaving them behind. I focus the telescope on the kids. "The Others," we called them then.

Mike Mullens, large and mean, hobbles through the meadow. His leg hasn't fully healed from the mukade bite he had gotten. Hans, the big blond dude follows him. And Carl. The only three left.

I don't feel sorry for them now. They swam out to sea to escape the *things*, and so they're still alive. Now they control the whole island.

I glance at Steffi. She faces the other way, towards the new island. Her red hair flutters in the breeze. I've been mad at her for the last two days, although I've tried hard to keep my anger hidden. I was angry because she wouldn't help me save those kids. Now I sigh and shove down my anger. She was right. Those guys, if we had rescued them, would make our lives a living hell.

"Breakfast?" I say, and she grins. We dive off the raft.

The cool seawater washes away the last traces of sleep. I take huge gulps of the stuff. Steffi, Rob, and I race to see who can swim around the canoe and rafts the fastest.

Soon everyone splashes in the cool water.

Back in our world, if you were stranded on a raft in a desolate sea, you wouldn't have much fun. You'd be starving, thirsty, sunburned, seasick and full of sores from the salty seawater. In this world, wherever this world is, the healing water relieves any burn we get, quenches thirst and satiates hunger. None of us have even gotten seasick. We could probably float this way until the end of time without ever getting sick, hungry, or thirsty, but the one thing the seawater can't cure is boredom. We have nothing to do and all day to do it.

Steve, the oldest, finally scrambles, dripping, onto a raft. He sits and kicks his feet in the water. "We need to think of some sort of plan," he says. "What are we gonna do when we reach that island? We can't fit any more kids on this boat. We can't save them."

"True," I say, "but we can immunize the kids to the mukade, if they aren't already. Then they can at least swim in the seawater. They'll have food and drink and they can escape the black things if they ever attack the island."

"So that's our plan?" Steffi says. "To stop at these islands, immunize everyone, and then head on?"

"I'm not sure what else we can do," I say.

We can't leave these people to suffer. We can at least make them more comfortable with their fate. But we aren't here to rescue them.

We're searching for something else. *Someone* else.

That someone lives on one of these islands, and I'm going to find him. That someone can tell us how to escape this planet and find our way home.

I don't say this out loud. It's a loopy idea, I have no proof to provide that there is such a person out there except my gut-feeling, and they aren't ready to hear that yet.

"We have one problem," Keiko says. "We're almost out of the black powder. The Others took the rest."

We had discovered the black powder when we found the telescope and Steffi's jeweled knife. Keiko figured out that it was an antidote for mukade bites. The wound would fester and refuse to heal if you didn't use the powder. We still have the vial. A thin layer of powder lies in the bottom.

Rob frowns. "Well, we have enough for the folks on the next island, maybe."

We splosh around until we're tired of swimming and lazily stroke back to the rafts. Steffi pulls herself onto the raft and sits next to Keiko. Her long legs trail in the water. She squints out to sea.

"What's that?"

I follow her pointing finger. Tiny ripples dance on the surface. Nothing unusual.

"I see it too. In the water, over there," Keiko says.

Spike flutters off the bow, peers across the water, and shrieks.

I'm beginning to *hate* the sound of bat shrieks. Whenever I hear them, something bad is always about to happen.

"Out of the water, now!" I yell. Everyone flounders for the nearest raft, which is the raft Keiko, Steve, and Steffi are already on.

"Other side, other side!" Steffi squeals. "You'll flip us if everyone gets on here!"

Nobody listens, they're too busy panicking. I steel myself and swim for the raft on the other side of the boat. A huge lump of ice bobs in my stomach. I don't breathe until I reach the raft and pull myself out of the water. Rob, Sarah, and Bhasker follow me. Our combined weight evens out the sides.

"It's getting closer!" Steffi yells.

I still don't see anything, but Steve points. A ripple. Tiny at first but growing as it heads straight towards us.

Right before it reaches the first raft, the ripple disappears. A second later the whole sea heaves, and the canoe and rafts bob skyward before slamming down on the sea. Bhasker screams as he flies off the raft and splashes into the churning water.

I stare, horrified, as he disappears.

THE ISLAND

I lunge forward and grab for Bhasker's hair. He bobs up, scream-ing. I get my hands under his armpits and heave him on the raft right as a huge green snout explodes into the air. Glistening white teeth snap wildly, missing Bhasker's toes by inches.

The monster doesn't attack the raft. Instead, it dives. A long, eely body whips through the depths. It turns and swims away.

"I think it's gone," I say.

"No," Steve says. "It's coming back this way."

We watch, unable to move, as the ripple glides towards us. Then Steve breaks the trance.

"Into the canoe! Everybody! Now!"

Long, skinny poles attach the flimsier rafts to the solid canoe. To reach the canoe, we must shimmy across the poles and hope we don't fall off, like Rob had this morning. The first wave from that monster had soaked the poles, and now they're slippery as hell.

Fear sticks us to the poles and gets us to the canoe. We fling ourselves in and fall on top of each other. Steve is right. We were *way* too vulnerable out on the raft.

The next wave hits. The rafts bobble but the canoe remains steady. As long as we lie on the bottom, we'll be okay.

Unless that thing decides to use its fangs to break apart the canoe.

We huddle together, barely daring to breathe. Another wave hits, and another, but eventually the bobbing stops. The creature, whatever it is, has given up.

We're safe. For now.

Spike lands on the bow and chirps in a soothing way.

"It's gone." I roll off a groaning Malika, who's been pinned under both me and Rob for the last five minutes.

Steffi sits up. "Well, I guess there *had* to be something nasty out there in this sea. It couldn't be all happy fishes and warm water."

"Did you see the size of that thing?" Rob says. "It could've crunched the whole boat with those jaws. Why didn't it?"

"Let's just be *glad* it didn't," Steve says, "and leave it at that."

Keiko peers over the canoe's side. "Oh, no," she whispers.

I follow her gaze, and something in my stomach plummets. One outrigger is skewed and half of one raft is floating away. We had lashed the rafts together with jungle grass and secured the outrigger to the rafts and canoe the same way. Some of the grass has frayed due to the monster's attack.

Rob and I grab the outrigger and straighten it while Steve lashes it to the canoe as best he can. Nobody wants to go after the floating raft poles. We watch as they drift away.

"Well," Steve says, trying to crack a smile. "Now we know the flaw in our design plan."

The beast doesn't return, but we're leery of the sea after that experience. Who knows what else is out there? Everyone's too scared to use the one good raft, which means eight of us are smooshed in the canoe. It's fifteen feet long by three feet wide, which doesn't give much room for anything except sitting with our knees squashed against our chests.

Tempers rise immediately.

"Can't you give me any more room?" Rob whines. He's stuck between Sarah and Steve, the two largest. Rob is no slouch himself. He stands at least six feet tall and has filled out considerably since the first time I met him. Back then, he was a sack of bones. Now, a nice layer of muscles covers those bones.

"Sorry," Sarah says, "but you have just as much room as anybody else."

"I should get more room than Bhasker or Malika," Rob says. "They're the smallest."

"We *do* have less room," Malika says. She is stuffed in the canoe's stern, where the space tapers to nothing. Bhasker has wedged his body into the bow, which tapers too.

"You know, we'd probably have more room if we put the supplies on the raft," Steffi says.

I shake my head. "Bad idea. One good wave and they'd be washed over the side."

Our supplies are scant. We don't need food or water, but the big metal pot, a couple of spears and axes Steve made, and some rocks for starting fires are stowed in the canoe, along with a supply of fruit for Spike and a wooden box containing the precious objects we found. A map. A journal. The telescope. The vial.

The knife doesn't stay in the box. Steffi keeps it in a jeweled scabbard strapped around her waist and doesn't let it out of her sight. That knife is worth all the rest of the objects put together. Until we found it, we couldn't shave, cut food, anything. We even used it to strip bark off trees. It never dulls and still glints in the light. Life would suck if we lost it.

So, there's nothing for it but for all of us, including the supplies, to stay crammed in the canoe. Our clothes finally dry, and the seawater fills our stomachs, but it doesn't do much for the cramped conditions or anybody's mood. Rob halfheartedly tries to lead everyone in a round of "Row-Row-Row Your Boat." Malika almost clocks him senseless with one of the oars for the mere suggestion.

<<<>>>

The new island stretches out in the darkness. It isn't mountainous and rocky like Mukade Island. It's flat and covered with an eerie blue glow. During the day, the glow disappeared and we observed that wavy purple grass blankets the entire island. Somewhere around the island's center, a mound rises. The purplish grass covers it as well. In fact, the whole island looks like one wavy, purple meadow.

"Much nicer than where we came from," Steve had said.

"I don't know," Steffi said. "I mean, can you imagine seeing the same thing day-in and day-out? Purple grass?"

Steve snorted. "I lived for three years seeing nothing but a rocky beach and spiny jungle. Until Jack came along and opened up the island for us, we only had a few square feet of space. You could never get comfortable, remember? The beach was rocky, the cave was rocky, and the jungle had those stupid sharp blades of grass we could never get through."

Now, as we near the shore, we stare at the island's glowing blue outline. "Why do you think it glows like that?" Steffi whispers.

"Dunno, but at least it'll be easier to see at night," I say. "Light's out was at least an hour ago, and I can still see the beach."

"I wonder where the kids on this island live," Rob says.

"Maybe they live in the center," Steve says. "On that mound."

"What about the mukade?"

I shrug. "I haven't seen any yet."

Rob peers at the island's outline. "Hey, wouldn't that be great if this island didn't *have* any mukade?"

Steve frowns as he watches a repulsive slug skitter down the beach. "It still has slugs. If it doesn't have mukade, what *does* it have? I bet it's got something horrible."

"Quit being such a killjoy," Steffi says. "Just 'cause our island sucked doesn't mean this one will."

11

We'd been close to shore most of the day, but we'd wanted to keep out of eyeshot. Steve worried the kids here might be like the kids we abandoned on Mukade Island. Mean and violent. Ready to ambush us if we let our guard down. If we land at night, we'll have plenty of time to scout out the island without worrying about possible problems from the natives.

As far as I can tell, the kids haven't stepped outside at night, which means they aren't immune to the mukade, if this island *has* mukade. If they dared step outside after dark, they'd be a quick mukade dinner.

Steve's comment gets me worried, though. What if this island *doesn't* have mukade? What if something lives here that we *aren't* immune to? Maybe landing at night isn't the brightest idea after all.

I push my uncertainty aside. "Well, we might as well land. See what we can find out."

Small waves roll into the shore, and the beach looks nice and sandy. This should be an easy landing. Steve, Rob, Sarah and I take the oars. We're the largest, although Steffi's probably stronger than me, to be honest. She works at it. Lifting rocks to gain muscle, doing sit-ups, that sort of thing. But she already rowed most of the afternoon.

The canoe and rafts scrape the sand, and we jump out, grateful to stretch our legs. We pull them up the sand, away from the lapping waves, and flop in the soft purple grass.

"What do we do now?" Malika asks.

"Let's scout the island out," Steve says. "It isn't big; half of us could go up the beach one way, half the other way, and we'll meet somewhere on the other side."

"Jack, you sure there's no mukade? Or anything else?" Rob asks.

"Just the kids," I say.

"We'd better careful," Bhasker says. "We don't know what other creatures might be out there. Remember the snakes from our island?"

I had never actually seen a snake on Mukade Island, but Malika shudders. "Okay, we'll be careful," I say. "Let's head out."

We break up and plow off in different directions. I take Steffi, Bhasker and Rob with me, and Steve, Keiko, Malika and Sarah head the other way.

We move slowly up the beach, avoiding, for now, the grassy middle.

"We could probably walk to the other side in a half hour or so," Steffi says. 'This island is way smaller than our own."

We walk for a bit, enjoying the soft sand and fresh breeze. I'm so glad to be off that boat. For the last two days, after that monster scared the hell out of us, we hadn't dared get in the water, even when we had lookouts posted. We lowered the pot over the side so everyone could have a drink and a wash. If we wanted to stretch, we'd stand and stretch as best we could, but nobody, even Steffi, who's braver than any of us, wanted to chance getting on the rafts.

We hadn't seen the sea creature since, though. The water had stayed calm and the sea floated us directly to this island. Like it knew this is where we wanted to go.

"What's that?" Bhasker, with his keen eyes, points to some low mounds off the beach to the right. We move to investigate. The lumpy ground here is free of grass. Something has been digging here.

Steffi freezes. "Is that an arm?"

I peer into the darkness, then turn around, a sick gurgle filling my stomach.

A pale arm pokes through one of the mounds, the skeletal fingers curved into a fist. Tattered flesh hangs off the bones. I gulp, trying to hold down my nausea.

Marissa.

We had found Marissa lying on the beach, the day before we left Mukade Island. She'd been half-eaten by the centipedes. We had dug a shallow grave and buried her, knowing it was a matter of time before the waves exposed her again.

Unless the mukade uncovered her first.

"You okay?" Steffi whispers. I know she is thinking of Marissa too.

"I'm fine," I say, even though I'm not.

"It's a graveyard," Rob says. "This is where they bury their dead."

"Or try to, anyway," Steffi says.

"Should we rebury that arm?" Rob asks. I can tell from his grimace he's hoping we'll say no.

Steffi sighs. "It wouldn't do much good. If there aren't any mukade here, something else is digging these graves up. And it'll just keep digging 'em up after we leave."

Bhasker shudders. "If it isn't mukade, then what?"

We move on. I'm glad the mounds are behind us, but shivers creep up my spine. That ghostly arm still sticks out of the sand, and in my mind, it starts to wave, beckoning us back to it. I resist the urge to bolt and force myself to think of the hand giving us the finger instead. That makes me laugh.

"What's so funny?" Rob asks.

"Nothing." I try to fight down the hysterics begging to break free. "God, can we run or something? Let's get away from that graveyard."

So we run. We pound up the beach, near the surf where the sand is firmer and the seawater washes over our feet. Nobody has shoes on except me, and mine are beginning to deteriorate. Everyone else's shoes disintegrated months ago.

"What are we attempting here, anyway?" Rob asks as we run.

"What do you mean?" I say between gasps. Sitting in the canoe for the last few days has really worn down my breathing ability. I can't believe I'm out of breath already.

"I mean, why are we stopping on this island? What can we do here? This isn't the way out. Aren't we looking for a way off this planet?"

"Well, for one, everyone was getting super cramped on that boat," I say, "and for two, we should help these kids out if we can."

"How many kids do you think are here?" Steffi asks.

"Just a few. I've seen maybe nine...ten."

"We don't have enough black powder to heal even that many," Rob says.

"Maybe not. But we have enough for some of them, and as long as a few kids can get immune to the seawater, life'll be better for the others. The immune kids can fish and stay out at night."

"But if there are no mukade, how will that will work?" Bhasker says.

"What do you mean?"

"I mean, on Mukade Island, a mukade had to bite us so we could become immune to the seawater. But if this island doesn't have any mukade, how will these kids become immune?"

I hadn't thought of that.

"And if they *do* get immune somehow, what if they want to come with us?"

"Of course they'll want to come with us, wouldn't you? But they can't. We'll just have to tell 'em that."

"Yeah, but what if they don't listen? What if they decide to sabotage us and take the canoe? We make 'em immune to seawater, they steal our one mode of transportation. They'll sneak away and leave us here."

I shake my head. "We have to assume that won't happen. That they'll be grateful for whatever we *can* give 'em."

"I don't think we should let them see the canoe. I think we should hide it," Rob says.

"They'll know we have a boat anyway, stupid," Steffi gasps as she slows to a walk. "How else would we have gotten here?"

"Well," Rob says, slowing down too, "we could tell them that we got transported here. You know, like what happens when kids first come to the islands. They just show up, right?"

"They'd never buy it," Steffi says. "Eight kids suddenly appearing all at once? Hell, on our island, it'd be months sometimes between kids showing up. And kids never show up eight at a time. Not even two at a time."

"Doesn't mean it couldn't happen," Rob says.

"Okay, say we did all appear here at once. What are the odds that we all know each other? We can't hide that fact from anyone. We can't pretend that we've just met."

"No," I say, "but we could pretend that we were from another island."

"We *are* from another island," Steffi says.

"Maybe we were on our island last night, but when we woke up, we were here."

"Like a prison exchange," Rob grins. "Somebody, whoever it is, decided to throw us all over here."

"Has that ever happened?" Bhasker asks.

"Even if it hasn't, why can't this be the first time? It'll explain why we're here and how we know each other. We can hide the canoe and rafts in the grass, in case we need to make a quick getaway. And nobody'll be the wiser."

"Unless they find it," Steffi says. "The whole island is flat and grassy. How can we hide a canoe and two rafts so nobody'd see 'em?

"Maybe we can put it in a safe zone," Rob says. "Far enough in the grass so the kids can't see it. If they can't get near enough to see it, they'll never know it's there."

"That's it," I say.

Steffi grins. "Yeah, and Rob of all people thought of it."

A safe zone. Back on our island, safe zones were scattered all over the place. Special places that, once a group of kids entered those areas, no other kids could come in. If it worked on Mukade Island, maybe a safe zone would work here too.

"I can't believe there'd be a spot on this island the native kids haven't been to yet," Bhasker says.

I glance at Spike. He chirps in my ear. Still a baby bat garble, but I think I can figure him out.

"What's he saying?" Bhasker whispers.

I grin. "What I thought he might say. Listen, on our island, the bats made the safe zones, and they also decided who could get into them. Those safe zones didn't even exist until the bats set them up."

"You think Spike could make us a safe zone here?" Steffi says.

"Well, he's still a baby, but he says he'll give it a go. He can probably make the area where we left the canoe into a safe zone. He doesn't think the kids have been in the grass."

"Boy, these bats are useful," Bhasker says.

"Makes you wonder why the kids *haven't* been in the grass," Steffi mumbles.

I nod at Spike. "You wanna go back there now and do it?"

But Spike doesn't. He suddenly shoots into the air and stares dead ahead.

Something moves towards us, down the beach. Something big.

Something that *isn't* a mukade.

THE TUNNEL

I can't decide if I should feel terror or calm. Spike's fluttering body is tense, but he hasn't started screeching yet. That's his usual *oh crap, it's time to panic* signal, and if he isn't panicking yet, I won't either.

Something glints in the dim light. Steffi holds the knife by her side, loose but ready to snap forward if she needs it. Rob carries a spear from the raft. That's all the protection we have.

The beast slinks into view, oozing a long trail of slime behind it. It snorts and slobbers as it approaches.

Steffi gulps. "What the hell *is* that?"

The huge creature's thick body pulses through the sand. A wide mouth opens and shuts. It must sense our presence, because I don't see any eyes. Like the mukade, this creature's vision is slim to none.

Whatever it is, it's larger than a mukade. It's like an over-grown walrus without any facial features except a gaping mouth. Everyone (and I'm ashamed to admit it, I do it too) hunkers behind Steffi and her knife.

"Babies." Steffi crouches and fixes her gaze on the moving blob.

"Is it dangerous?" Bhasker whispers.

Spike still hasn't screeched yet. He flutters around, sizing this new creature up. Trying to figure it out.

The thing yawns. Long, pointy fangs glint in the darkness.

"I don't like the looks of that," Steffi says.

"Neither do I," Bhasker says. "Let's get out of here."

I'm all for that idea. But then Spike does something I don't expect. He coos.

I've never heard the sound come out of a bat before. It's like he's talking in some different language. The creature shuts its huge mouth and tilts what I assume to be its head, but it's hard to tell. The thing doesn't really have much shape.

"Maybe it's a worm," Rob whispers.

"Worms don't have teeth," Steffi says.

"Neither do slugs, not in our world anyway. But the slugs here have teeth. Maybe worms do too."

"If that's a worm, it's a worm from hell," Steffi says. "Look at the size of it. It's bigger than a car."

Spike flutters around the worm, still cooing in his singsong voice, then flies back to me. "It's friendly," I say as the worm lumbers past us. "Well, not super-friendly, but it definitely isn't an enemy. Spike says it digs tunnels. It told Spike where one of the entrances is."

"Why on Earth should we go into that thing's tunnels?" Bhasker says.

I shrug. "Spike thinks we should. Apparently, that thing has made tunnels all through the island. Spike says the worm is off to find its dinner. It eats slugs and grass, apparently."

"Poor slugs," Steffi says. "They can't get a break anywhere."

Bhasker frowns. "It sure has pointy teeth. Why does it need such pointy teeth to eat grass?"

"Spike says it uses the teeth to chew up dirt and make the tunnels."

Rob stares at the little bat. "It still amazes me that you can get all that information from a couple of chirps."

It amazes me too. Spike's garbled baby talk is making more and more sense. He learns fast. I wonder how he knew the worm wouldn't be a danger to us. And how he figured out how to talk to it.

I'll probably never know. All I know is that the bats learn as they go. They enter an environment and soak up everything about it, like osmosis. They learn from their surroundings; they don't have to be taught anything.

Spike is only a few months old, but already he's figured out this new place. He's never seen a worm like that before, but he understands how to communicate with it. He's an amazing little creature.

"Why should we explore tunnels right now?" Steffi asks.

I turn to Spike for the answer. He chirps.

"Because," I say, "there's something in there we need to find."

<<<>>>

The tunnel's entrance hides behind a clump of tall grass. It's wide and dark and earthy. Not at all like the rocky tunnels on Mukade Island. Definitely made by a living thing. Thick white strings of some shimmery substance hang around the opening.

"What are those, do you think?" Bhasker asks, reaching out and poking one. "Ow!"

He pulls his finger back, the glimmering string sticking to it like glue.

"Damn it, that *stings*." Bhasker shakes his hand until the string pops free from the earthy soil. It still clings to his hand, though.

"Try washing it off with seawater," Steffi suggests. "That might get it off."

Bhasker gallops towards the beach, the string trailing after him. "You think that worm thing made that stuff?" Steffi says, watching him go. "Maybe it's like a bloated silk worm or something."

I shrug and stick my head into the tunnel entrance, careful to duck under the wavering strands. "It's sure dark in there."

"I don't know about this," Rob says. "That worm thing was huge. Maybe it's trying to lure us in there."

I shake my head. "I don't think so."

"Hey, you don't think it's a slug, do you? I mean, it isn't pink like the slugs, but it has a mouth like one. Maybe that's the Queen Slug."

Steffi laughs. "The what?"

"You know, like how bees have a Queen Bee. What if this is the Queen Slug? What if that tunnel is full of tons of little worker slugs with sharp little teeth?"

"Stop letting your imagination run away with you, Rob," Steffi says. "That thing didn't look anything like a slug."

"Neither do Queen Bees. But they're still bees."

Bhasker rejoins us. "That worked. It dissolved as soon as I dunked my hand in the seawater. Got rid of the sting, too."

Spike flies in first. We follow, but lose the dim light a few feet in. We didn't bring any torches with us.

"We aren't gonna get far if we can't see where we're going," Steffi says.

Spike flits back and grabs my hair, like Pepe the bat used to do on Mukade Island. It's crazy, but as soon as the little bat's claws touch my hair, I get instant night-vision. A green light fills the tunnel. The passage veers to the right and out of sight.

"I'll go on alone," I say. "You guys stay here."

"Bad idea," Steffi says. "We should stick together."

"I'll be fine."

"You don't know that," Rob says. "You don't know what else is down there. Here, take my spear at least. We'll be okay with Steffi's knife."

Bhasker shivers. "No, we won't. I don't like this. We won't have the bat or the spear if you leave. What if that worm comes back and decides humans are tasty snacks after all?"

I look at Spike. He chirps. There's nothing he can do. He can't provide light for everyone.

"Will you scout it out for us?" I ask.

Spike chirps an assent and flies down the tunnel. The green light disappears. We move outside and wait.

"Let's take a swim while we wait for Spike," Steffi says.

We peel off our clothes and run into the lapping sea. I doubt any huge monsters will get this close to shore. The seawater washes off the last couple days of sweat and accumulated grime.

Steffi pulls out first. I try to keep my eyes averted as she moves back up the beach to grab her clothes and the knife.

Rob shoots me a grin. "You've seen her naked a million times before, Jack. What gives?"

"He's embarrassed," Bhasker says.

"I'm not embarrassed."

Rob laughs. "Yeah, sure you're not."

"The bat is back," Steffi yells.

Spike has flown the entire length of the tunnel. He says that it cuts across the island and ends at the other side. The tunnel might be dark, but it's smooth and wide. So we elephant-train it. I go first, with Spike's claws latched onto my hair. Steffi keeps her hand on my shoulder, Rob holds on to Steffi, and Bhasker clings to Rob. We move through the tunnel, slow but safe.

The tunnel is warm and smells pleasant, not at all like how I thought a worm hole would smell. Especially a worm that secretes ooze as it moves, like that one did.

We move steadily forward for several minutes. The tunnel turns this way and that, but it stays wide and even, sloping gently down then up again. We reach a place where the tunnel widens into a room. The worm's bedroom, by the looks of it. A great nest of fluffed grass is piled in one corner. I can see several tunnels in the green light, exiting the chamber in different directions.

A wooden box lies in one corner of the room. I gasp and bolt for it.

"Hey!" Steffi yells, her voice echoing off the walls. "Where are you going?"

"Sorry! I'm over here. Follow my voice. It's a box, Steffi!"

"A box?"

"Yeah, like the one we found in the cavern on Mukade Island. The box with the treasures. It's the same thing."

Steffi moves my way. "Crazy. Somebody's stashing stuff on these islands on purpose? Why?"

"I don't know, but it's bound to have some cool things in it." I run my hand over the rough wood. "Give me your knife. I can't use the spear; its blade is too thick. We can get the knife in between the slats and pry it open."

Steffi hands it reluctantly over. "Don't bend it."

I can't help laughing. "Steffi, we've hacked half of our canoe into existence using this knife. It doesn't bend."

Still, I have to wrestle with the box a bit before the lid pops off. I stare inside.

"What's in it?" Rob says. "Any more of that powder stuff in there?"

"I don't know. Quit crowding." My hand closes around something and I pull it out. Large, round and flat, it glints in the dim light.

"It looks like a shield or something," I say.

I hand it to Steffi and pull out the next object. A leather pouch. I open it and pull a long chain out. Small bells dangle off the chain. They give off a beautiful tinkling sound as I wave them in the air.

"What do you think the bells are for?" Rob says.

"I don't know."

"What else?" Steffi asks.

An axe. Solid, but light. I pull it out of its leather case. The blade is flat and sharp. That will come in handy. Too bad we didn't have it when we were building our canoe.

"Who gets it?" Rob asks, when I tell them what it is.

"What do you mean?"

"I mean, Steffi got to keep the knife. Who gets the axe? 'Cause I want it. I want a weapon."

"You'll hack your arm of with it," Steffi says.

"No, I won't."

"We don't need to decide who gets it now." I rummage through the box. A thin roll of paper lies on the bottom. I grab it and unroll it.

"It's a map," I say.

"Another one?" Steffi asks. "The map we have shows every detail of our island. Maybe this map shows this island."

"It wouldn't need to show much," Bhasker says. "You can see the whole island from the boat."

"Maybe it shows where the worm's tunnels go," I say. "There's quite a few tunnels leading away from here."

I roll it up. There's nothing else in the box, so we put the lid back on. Steffi carries the shield, Bhasker has the bells. We let Rob carry the axe. Spike chirps and leads us forward.

"Not a bad night's work," Steffi says. "Should we go back the same way?"

Spike chirps. "He says this tunnel over here heads to the other side of the island, where Steve and the others went. If we go this way, we'll probably catch up with them."

We trudge up the new tunnel until we reach the exit, which is covered with more shimmery strands.

"This is going to hurt," Bhasker says. "Maybe we should go back."

"No, let's just bolt through 'em," Steffi says. "C'mon."

She dives towards the exit. The strands hook to her hair and arms like little gripping tentacles. She doesn't scream like Bhasker did. She books to the water and dives in.

Steffi's mad dash has cleared most of the strands away, so the rest of us exit unscathed. Rob nods towards four shadows tromping up the beach. Steve, Keiko, Sarah, and Malika. "Let's sneak up on 'em."

We jog through the sand but don't get far before Steve whips around, terror on his face.

Rob grins. "Just us."

"Damn it, don't do that again! You scared the hell out of me. We almost got eaten by a huge worm-thing..."

Rob laughs. "He wasn't anything to worry about. He's dug tunnels all through this place. Look what we found." He waves the axe around.

"Rob, you're gonna slice someone's head off," Steffi says, jogging up to meet us.

"We found another box, Steve," I say.

Steve's eyes widen. "Are you serious?'

I nod. "Down in the tunnel."

"Well," Steve says, "you've had a bit more of an adventure than we've had. All we've seen, besides the worm, is beach, slugs, and grass."

"Seen any mukade?"

"Nope. Not one. I think you're right. This island doesn't have any."

"We should find where the kids live," Sarah says. "They must live in that mound somewhere." She motions to the hill covered with wavering grass.

I stare at the dark hill. Spike chirps into my ear, and I shudder.

"He says it isn't safe," I say. "We should wait on the beach until light."

"Does something bad live up there?" Rob asks.

"I don't know. I don't think Spike does either, but as long as we stay along the outskirts of it we're fine. Once we get into that grass though..."

I leave the sentence unfinished as a blood-curdling scream shatters the silent night.

ANANSI

Steffi draws her knife. Rob holds the axe out and flails the air in front of him. I grab tight to the spear. Steve has one too.

"Stop that!" he hisses at Rob. "You're gonna disembowel one of us if you keep that up."

"What *is* it?" Rob whispers. Even in the dark I can see the whites of his eyes. I can't blame him for his fear. That scream was inhuman, piercing. My insides turn to ice, and I pray that whatever made it stays where it's at and doesn't come investigate us. It didn't sound like a fearful scream. No, it sounded more like rage.

Or hunger.

Spike flutters, head cocked towards the diminishing sound. He doesn't know what it is either.

"Spike," I whisper. "Now might be a good time for a safe zone."

"Can he make one anywhere?" Steve asks.

"I don't know. He can't make one around us now, while we're standing on this beach. He needs boundaries. The safe zones on Mukade Island had some definition. Like the room in the cave, or the path through the jungle. Or the glade. There were edges to them. If he tried to make a safe zone here, he'd have to make the whole beach a safe zone, and that'd take forever. If he could even do it."

"What about the worm's tunnel?" Rob says. "Could he transform that?"

Steffi shivers. "Even if he can't, let's get into it. I'd rather be in there than out here."

We backtrack to the tunnel and creep inside the entrance. Spike chirps.

"He's gonna try it now," I say.

"But won't that block the worm out?" Bhasker says. "If Spike makes this a safe zone, the worm can't use it."

"Can't he make it so us *and* the worm can use the tunnel?" Rob asks.

I shrug. "I don't know."

"Poor Spike," Malika says. "He's never made a safe zone before, and we're asking him to start with a complicated one."

Spike scrambles along the wall and sniffs. He definitely is going to give it a go.

Another scream echoes into the tunnel. Whatever makes it has gotten closer. Keiko lets out an involuntary yelp. Bhasker and Malika huddle next to Sarah, who blocks them with her big frame. Steve and Steffi stand closest to the entrance, guarding it. Rob cowers behind them. His axe wobbles dangerously in his hands.

Then I see it.

Long, hairy legs. A huge body. Glinting eyes. Sharp, clicking fangs.

A spider unlike any I've ever seen. It's so enormous I doubt it can fit its body into the tunnel. It scuttles around the entrance, peers in, and pokes a hairy, spiky leg into the tunnel. Then the horrifying thing draws its leg back and hisses in pain and anger.

"Whatever Spike is doing, it's working," Steve says.

Malika doesn't care. She screams and bolts down the dark tunnel. The others scramble after her. I'm too transfixed by those huge, waving legs to follow. The spider shoves its mouth as close as it can to the tunnel and screams.

The piercing sound amplifies through the tunnel and hits me like a foul wind, breaking me from my trance. I bolt after the others, zoom around a bend, and slam into Rob. We lie in a groaning pile.

In her blind scramble, Malika must have smashed into the wall, and the others piled up behind her. At least we're around the bend and can't see that horrible monster anymore. We can still hear it, though.

"Is everyone okay?" I gasp over the spider's horrific wail.

"Make it stop!" Malika screams.

"It isn't coming in," Steffi says. "Rob, put the axe away before you chop off somebody's arm."

Malika calms down. We disentangle from each other.

"Thanks Spike," I whisper. The bat flutters along the wall and chirps.

"He's made a safe zone from the entrance to the next bend," I say.

"And it works," Rob says. "Not bad for a baby bat."

"What do we do now?" Malika says.

"We stay here," Steve says, "until that thing goes away."

"It won't leave until daybreak, I bet," I say, "but at least we're safe here. For now."

<<<>>>

The worm visits us right when daylight clicks on. We recognize his grunts as he shifts through the sand. I chance a peek around the tunnel's bend.

"Spider's gone," I say, "but he's left his calling card. Look at the entrance. It's blocked shut with those shimmery strings."

"So it was a spider's web," Bhasker says, shivering. "Ugh."

I can barely make out the worm's shadow on the other side of the web. Then it thrusts its mouth in, its long teeth making short work of the silvery strands. Now only a couple dangle from the roof as the worm scoots in through the hole. The sticky, stingy web seems to have no effect on it.

"Well, at least the worm can still get in," I say as Malika cowers behind Rob.

"What *is* that thing?" she whispers.

"It's okay, he's friendly," Rob says.

She peers over his shoulder. "As long as he's not like Anansi."

"Who?"

"Anansi. The monster spider. You have never heard of Anansi?"

"Nope. Is that what they call spiders in Africa?"

Malika gulps. "Anansi is the spider spirit." She shudders.

"Well, it looks like Anansi might be afraid of our worm friend," Steffi says. "He must be gone anyway, for the worm to get through." She shoots a friendly smile at the large blob. The worm yawns at her, displaying his sharp white teeth. Malika ducks behind Rob again.

"Are you sure that thing is safe?" she whispers.

"If it weren't, it'd have eaten us already." I mimic the worm's yawn. I'm suddenly super-sleepy. I haven't closed my eyes since last night. We rowed all day and explored all evening. The confrontation with Anansi has worn me out.

I slump to the floor and rest my back against the smooth tunnel wall.

I mean to close my eyes for a minute, but when I open them, the others are gone except Bhasker who snores next to me, his head propped against my shoulder. The weapons and treasures are still stacked against the wall. I shake the boy awake.

"They must be out on the beach, getting breakfast," I say. "Come on."

The waves feel like heaven, so warm and soothing, and we drink and splash and float on our backs until Steffi taps my shoulder. "They're here."

I turn my eyes to the shore. A group of kids stand on the beach, staring at us with wide eyes and open mouths.

<<<>>>

There's a stark difference between these kids and the kids I observed when I first landed on Mukade Island. For one, they sure don't look like they're starving. They're fat and healthy. But there's a haunted, jumpy look in their eyes, and after meeting up with that ginormous spider last night, I can understand why. The kids don't seem menacing. They're mostly scared.

Steffi gives them a pert wave. A couple of the kids begin to raise their hands but then think better of it and lower them.

"Should we go talk to them?" Rob asks.

"Well, we can't stay in the water all day," Steffi says. "And Jack made us stop here for a reason: to help these kids out, although they don't much look like they need it. But I guess we'd better get on with it."

We count ten, mostly kids. One or two are older; they've managed to stay alive longer than most. The group shrinks away from us as we plow towards shore. None of them are bold, like Steffi was when I first met her. I scrutinize them more closely and notice something else. Although they're definitely not malnourished like we were, something seems wrong with each of them. One kid limps. One squints like he can hardly see us. One kid has a stump where his arm should be.

The squinting guy must be the leader. At least I think he's the leader. He's the only one brave enough to step forward and meet us. I'd guess he's a year or two older than Steve. He might've been handsome once, but now he sports a tangled beard and hair so long I can barely make out his watery blue eyes. He stumbles to us and sticks out a hand.

"Hi," he says. "I'm Frank Mullens."

I gulp. "Did you say *Mullens*?"

The guy squints at me. "Do I know you?"

"Yeah...I think we lived on the same street. I'm Jack Jones."

"Holy crap...Jack?" Frank's mouth breaks into a grin, and he takes a step forward. Two of his teeth are missing. "I'm sorry, I can't see your face very well."

"Are you blind?" Rob asks.

"Almost. Lost my glasses a while ago. My eyesight sucks. I don't come out of the cave much, can't risk it, but when Nadia said she saw new kids, I had to come out and see for myself. Well, try to see, anyway."

Steffi glances from Frank to me. "Wait...is this Mike's brother? They've got the same last name."

She looks uneasy. I understand. Mike Mullens was bad enough, and she's afraid this guy might be cut from the same cloth. But I remember Frank. Unlike the idiot Mike, Frank had some brains in his head. He tutored me in algebra when I was younger. He was always kind to me.

He turns his watery, hopeful eyes towards Steffi. "You know Mike? Is he here too?"

Steffi chews a nail and shrugs. She doesn't want to answer.

"He's on our island," I say. "Mukade Island. The island we left."

The little girl with the limp sways and frowns. "There's other islands?"

Frank ignores her. "Is Mike...is he okay?"

I don't want to discuss Mike Mullins. Not now.

"He's fine," I say. Frank looks relieved to hear these words.

"He didn't come with you?"

"No...uh...some of us didn't make it. But he's okay."

"So, you don't have any mukade here?" Steffi asks.

Frank frowns. "Mukade?"

"Sorry. Centipedes. Big, fat ones. Our island was covered with 'em."

Frank shakes his head. "No, no centipedes. Just the spider. And thank God there's only one of those."

"Yeah, we'd better hurry up and get some grub, Frank," one of the other kids says. "You never know when it'll come back out."

"Even in the daytime?" Malika asks, glancing up the beach.

31

Frank nods. "He's less active right around midday, but sometimes he shows up, just to keep us on our toes. Sometimes we can appease him with slugs, if we kill enough of 'em. He likes those. But...he likes the taste of human even more."

"And we aren't immune to *that*," Rob whispers in my ear. "He had no problem chasing us last night."

"We'd better be moving, Frank," the kid with the one arm says. "It's well after midday."

Frank nods. "We're off to gather food. Come with us. We try to do it when Pooky is at his sleepiest."

Rob grins. "Pooky?"

Frank's face gets a little red. "The spider. Some girl named him a couple of years ago. She figured maybe we wouldn't be as scared if he had a cute name. But it didn't help much. That poor kid became Pooky's lunch a few days later."

He says this with a toneless voice I'm fast becoming used to. It's how the kids on our island talked of somebody who'd died. Flat. No emotion. Like the victim wasn't human to begin with. Steffi says it's to distance ourselves from the horror. But man, I hate it when someone uses that tone.

"Pooky," Steve mutters.

"Well, the name stuck anyway," Frank says. "We usually have a few day's supply of food stored up, but we've eaten most of it, so now's the time to restock. The orchard is this way. C'mon."

The "orchard" lies on the island's far side. It isn't a true orchard with trees, it's more a grubby collection of low bushes laden with fist-sized yellow fruit. On our way to the orchard, we pass a large round stone partially hiding a tunnel entrance.

"What's that?" I ask Frank, pointing to the stone as I trudge beside him. He squints and follows my finger.

"Oh, that's our cave. It's where we live. Fairly safe from Pooky, although every once in a while he tries to get in. Over there, running through the orchard, is the only fresh water we've got."

"And is the orchard your only food source?" Rob says.

Frank nods. "The fruit is pretty tasty, although I could sure go for something else just to break the monotony. The bushes never seem to run out of 'em, although we pick loads to eat."

"Well, you've got the slugs too," Steffi says.

Frank makes a face. "Why on Earth would we want to eat those? They're Pooky food, not people food. We only collect 'em as a sacrifice to the Spider God." He grins at his own joke.

We reach the bushes and begin picking the golden fruit. They look like plums but taste like strawberries. The kid with the one arm sidles up to me and reaches his only hand towards a loaded branch. "How did you escape your island?" he asks.

"More importantly, how can you swim in the sea?" Frank says. "It burns us if we touch it. We never usually venture down the beach, but one of the kids spotted you when we were about to head for the orchard."

Our original idea last night was to cover up our escape with little lies. But now, as we pick the fruit, we tell them our story. Of how, on our island, we figured out that if a mukade bites us, we become immune to the poisonous sea. And drinking the seawater made the mukade fear us and stay as far away as possible.

"What did you do before that?" one of the younger boys pipes up. "Before you became immune to the mukade? How did you keep them away?"

"Well, our cave was a safe zone, of course," I say.

"A what?"

"A safe zone. You know, the mukade couldn't come in."

The kids stare at each other, bewilderment on their faces.

"You mean you don't have that here?" Sarah asks.

"A safe zone? No," Frank says. "We're always on guard for the spider. Sometimes it attacks our shelter at night. We keep that large rock across the entrance, but even so, sometimes it tries. Somebody always has to be there for lookout."

"And it'll try to block our entrance with its stinging web," the limping girl says. "That's always a pain to get through. Get it? Pain?" She grins.

"They don't have a bat," Rob whispers to me. "The bats made the safe zones on our island right?"

"Does that spider crawl around here every night?" Steve asks. "Is it the only one?"

"The only one we've ever seen," Frank says. "It lives up in the tall grass. If we kill enough slugs and leave them on the beach, sometimes it'll eat those and leave us alone. But sometimes we hear it, scraping at the rock. Sometimes it manages to move the rock, and we have to push back to make sure it can't reach us. But sometimes we'll hear a roar. Not a scream, like the spider gives, but a deep roar. And then, the spider will go away. Whatever makes the roar scares it off."

Rob nods. "The worm."

Frank gives him a perplexed look. "What?"

"The huge one with the big teeth that made those tunnels in the hill. We ran into him last night."

Frank drops a fruit in amazement. "I've been here five years, and I've never even *seen* it. Not that I could with my craptacular eyesight, but *nobody* here has seen it. We knew there must be something else on this island, but it never comes out during the day. Sometimes we hear weird things at night, like grunts and stuff, sounds that don't sound like the spider."

"The worm grunts," Rob says.

Frank shakes his head. "You guys know more about this island than we do, and you just got here."

"That's 'cause we've had the absolute joy of creeping around it at night," I say, remembering how cock-sure of ourselves we were when we first landed. We were hoping for mukade. Harmless, fear-filled mukade. How wrong we were.

Spike chirps.

"Let's head back to your shelter," I say to Frank.

"But we haven't picked enough fruit yet," one of the smaller kids says. "And we need to catch some slugs. Pooky'll be out soon."

"Not all of you have to go," I say. "But we can make that shelter a safe zone, right now. If you show us where it is."

"I'll go back with you," Frank says. "I can't help much out here, I can hardly see my hand in front of my face."

We head up the beach. Frank and a skinny kid named Matt escort Steve, Keiko and me to the shelter. Steffi stays with the rest to help gather fruit. Rob, Bhasker, Sara and Malika say they'll gather seaweed and maybe catch some fish, to give Frank and the others some much-craved variety to their diets.

The shelter is a shoveled-out hole in the ground. It has the same slick walls the worm's tunnel had. Nice and hard, but the comforting earthy smell is missing. Instead, an acrid urine odor invades my nostrils, so heavy with ammonia I want to gag. I smell poo too, but at least that's been cleaned out. These kids don't have any kind of toilet. They must piss in a corner and live with the smell. Or hold it until they dare sneak outside.

The inside is pretty cramped. I'm amazed that ten kids can even smush in here. The heavy gray rock, the only stone I've seen so far on this island, is positioned near the entrance.

"It takes four of us to push it shut," Frank says.

"You won't have to anymore, once Spike is done," I tell him.

"What about the orchard?" Keiko says. "Can Spike make that a safe zone too?"

"I bet he can. That would make sense, since that's the main food and water supply. Spike?"

Spike chirps his assent and flitters out the cave entrance. We follow. "You stay in here, Frank, where it's safe," Matt says. "We'll be back in a jiffy."

"Are you sure the cave is safe now?" Frank says. "It doesn't seem like the bat actually *did* anything."

"Oh, he did. Trust me." I step outside and scan the area for the spider, but don't see anything. "When does...um, Pooky usually make an appearance?"

"Right about now," Matt, says following my gaze. "It's getting late in the afternoon. He doesn't sleep much. We're running late today."

We head to the orchard so Spike can continue his work. A small stream flows between the fruit bushes and out to the beach. The stream has eaten into the sandy soil, creating a shallow ditch. Its clear water smells sweet, even from a distance.

"How do you collect the water?" I say.

"Here." Matt hands me a bowl that looks like glass but feels like plastic.

"Where'd you get this?"

"We found it on the beach. Every once in a while, we'll dig these up in the sand. I'm not sure what kind of animal makes 'em. They're perfect for collecting fruit and water."

He fills up the bowl as Spike flies up the creek, sniffling.

"He can use the orchard boundary to make the safe zone," I say. "Thanks, Spike."

Matt watches the bat flitter around the orchard and then head back to us. "What does it mean?"

"It means Pooky can't get into these areas anymore. If you're in your shelter or in this stream, or even picking fruit in the orchard, he can't touch you."

"I don't believe you," Matt says.

I don't blame him for his skepticism, but a "thank you" would still be nice to hear. But he doesn't say anything else. He stares at me with solemn brown eyes.

"Well, that's done anyway," Steve says, sounding more annoyed than me at Matt's lack of gratitude.

I stare out at the beach where Rob, Bhasker, Sarah, and Malika have made a pile of seaweed and fish. A couple of the island kids hover around them, staring with wonder at the plentiful catch, I step out on the beach, with the intention of helping them lug all their bounty to the cave. It's a pretty nice beach, much nicer than our old rocky one. Nothing but warm white sand and crashing waves. The orange sea sparkles in the sunlight. In a way, this place is much nicer than Mukade Island.

But in a way, just as horrendous.

The spider bursts from the waving purple grass and pounces towards the kids on the beach. Long, flailing legs thrust its huge, bloated torso through the sand. It eats up the distance between its pincers and the nearest juicy kid.

Pooky is on the hunt.

DESTRUCTION

I can already tell that all the kids won't make it back. They're running as hard as they can, but the spider is faster. It doesn't even slow down for the mound of slugs lying in the sand. I stare in horror as the great, scuttling monster nears the limping girl who lags at the back of the pack. Her face is frozen in terror. I can't stand to watch.

But I can't wait while something horrible happens. I grip my spear. "Come on!" I yell at Rob as I charge towards the oncoming crowd. I don't know what I expect to happen, but my mind is filled with an all-encompassing rage birthed out of the all-consuming fear I had felt minutes before. I don't know if Rob is following me or not. All I see is that poor girl, now so petrified she's almost at a stand-still.

Steffi, always the fastest, sprints past me and pulls out her knife. She rushes past the girl. Now Steffi stands in the way of Pooky and his victim.

Of course that means now *she's* the victim.

All of a sudden the horrific beast stops. It skids backwards, all ten legs (I counted) flailing wildly as it tries to scramble back the way it came. We slow, watching the horrible spider morph from an angry monster into a quickly retreating scar-dy-cat. It lumbers into the grass, heading for its lair. Instead of the bloodcurdling screams, a high, frantic wheezing exits its jaws.

"He's scared," Rob says, breathing hard next to me. He flails the axe around, and I take a couple of steps away from his arm range. "Like the mukade when we got too close. But he didn't do that last night. He wasn't afraid of us at all, then."

"I can't believe we scared that thing off so easily," Steffi says. "It's gotta be something else."

I look at Spike who's followed us, but he doesn't know why Pooky ran the other way. I turn around. Sarah and Steve have joined us. Steve has the extra spear, but Sarah is weaponless.

"Why'd you follow us with no weapon?" I ask.

She shrugs. "I dunno. Gut reaction I guess. I saw you guys running this way and I didn't even stop to think that I didn't have anything to protect myself with except this." She waves the shield in the air. "Stupid huh?" She grins.

I smile back. Sarah is nothing if she isn't brave.

"I'd sure like to know why Pooky ran from us," I say.

Steffi laughs. "Pooky?"

"He wasn't scared of us last night," Steve says. "Maybe there's something different we're doing now. But what?"

"Well, he's gone for now," Sarah says. "And the kids are safe in their shelter. What should we do now?"

"We've got seaweed and some fish," Malika says. "We should bring those to the kids."

"You guys go," I say. "I'd like to take Spike back to the canoe. We need to figure out how to make a safe zone around it, so nobody can get to it but us."

Everyone agrees. Steve, Steffi, and I head to the canoe. We decide to wade the distance, as far off-shore as we can get, under the hopeful assumption that Pooky can't swim. The rest head back to feed the kids.

"What a crappy island," Steve says. "I'll be glad when we get off it."

"I dunno," Steffi says. "Seems much nicer here than Mukade Island. A sandy beach, fresh water, all the fruit you can eat...all you have to do is watch out for one big, fat spider."

Steve shudders. "I hate spiders. Give me a mukade any day. I can't wait to leave."

"We will soon," I say. "We've given the kids a safe zone; if Spike could set up a few more for them, then we'll have done all we can."

"We can't do anything about Pooky though," Steffi says. "They'll always have to live with that horror. And there's no way I see to immunize the kids against the seawater."

"Unless Pooky has to bite them to get 'em immune," Steve says.

Steffi shudders. "I don't think *anyone* would survive that."

The canoe lies ahead. I spot the top of it behind a rise in the beach. Spike flies up in the air and gives a surprised chirp. I freeze.

"What now?" Steffi says.

"The canoe. Oh hell."

I start swimming, hard—a sick sensation spreading through my gut. I scramble out of the water, reach the top of the rise, and suck in my breath.

The canoe lies in pieces, scattered in the grass.

Ruined.

"What the *hell*?" Steffi erupts out of the water and plows through the sand towards the broken canoe.

The main hull is intact, but the outriggers have been torn apart and flung about, the raft poles scattered. Our belongings—the box, cup, pot, and backpack—litter the beach.

"What did this?" Steve says.

"One guess," Steffi answers. "Anansi. Pooky. Whatever you want to call him. He's left his calling card." She points to shimmery white strands covering the wreckage.

Rob groans. "How are we gonna clean all that stuff off?"

Steffi grimaces and pries the pot and cup loose. She curses as she bolts into the sea to clean them off. "Damn it, that stings."

"Thanks, Steffi," Rob says, looking a little guilty at not having the guts to grab the utensils himself.

"You're welcome." She throws the pot towards Rob's chubby belly. "Start washing."

She and Rob traipse back and forth, filling up the cup and pot and washing the web off the canoe while Steve and I watch out for Pooky. After an hour, all the spider gunk is gone.

"I sure hope we can put the canoe and rafts back together," Steve says.

"We've lost some poles," Rob says. "Pooky must've taken them back to his nest."

"Damn, you're right." Steve scrutinizes the poles that are left. "Not enough for even one raft."

"Worse, one of the outriggers is broken," I say. Half of one outrigger lies in the sand, The other half is gone.

"We *need* that piece," Steve says. "It's the strongest part. We can't leave without it."

Steffi shudders. "We'll have to hunt down Pooky to get it."

Rob sighs and flings himself down in the sand. "What's the use? We can't put it back together. We're screwed."

We stare at the broken canoe. My heart sinks. Rob is right. This island doesn't have the resources we need. We need wood, and not one tree grows on this rock. Only the bushes in the orchard and lots and lots of purple grass.

"Okay," Steffi says, "let's not dwell on that now. We've gotta get this boat into a safe zone and save what's left."

Steve scans the beach. "Where can Spike set up a safe zone?"

"Why don't we clear an area in the grass?" Steffi says. "We can make a small circle, enough to stash the canoe and its pieces in."

It takes most of the afternoon, but we manage to yank up the thick grass and clear an area wide enough to put the canoe. By the time we've moved all the bits and pieces into the circle, and Spike has flown around the entire area, doing whatever he does to make it into a safe zone, Keiko and Sarah make their way to us.

"Thank God you're okay," Sarah says. "The lights are about to click off, and we thought you might have had a run-in with Pooky." She halts. "What happened to the boat?"

"The spider got to it," Steve says.

Keiko frowns. "Does this mean we're stuck here?"

"Until we figure out how to fix it, yes," Steve says. "I'm afraid we are."

<<<>>>

The hovel where the kids on this island live isn't big enough for them and us. I wouldn't want to sleep there anyway: the urine smell is too overwhelming and the cave is way too crowded. We move our camp to the worm's tunnel. Spike has already made it a safe zone, so it makes sense.

"We *aren't* peeing in it," Steffi says.

"We can't go outside at night though," Rob says. "Not with Pooky prowling around. What if we have to go to the bathroom in the middle of the night?"

"Hold it 'till morning," Steffi says.

"What if we can't?"

"Learn how."

We sit in the tunnel and wait for the daylight to switch off. Everyone's in a bad mood. Knowing we're stuck here has sucked the happiness out of us. At least the kids that live here have benefited. We lugged most of the grass we had pulled back to their cave so the island kids could make a roaring fire. They're happy with the new circumstances.

We are not.

"They have it pretty easy, if you think about it," Steffi says. "All the fruit they can eat, a nice beach to lounge around

42

on, when the spider isn't lurking about, and sweet water to drink."

"Yeah, but it's weird, isn't it?" Rob says. "I mean, did you notice that every one of those kids has some kind of defect?"

Steve frowns. "I used to have a 'defect'."

"Yeah, but you didn't come from our world with it. I talked to a couple of those kids. They all had their defects back on Earth. Frank has really bad eyesight. Matt has epilepsy and seizes up at weird times. Aaron...that's the kid with only one arm...he lost it in a car accident when he was four. The little girl with the limp, Nadia, was born with it."

"So?" Steve says.

"So...isn't it weird? Mukade Island was a lot tougher, but we were stronger. Here, except for Pooky, everything is easy. But these kids don't have good defenses against that spider, do they?"

Rob can be so observant sometimes. "It's like they're livestock," I say.

Steffi frowns. "What?"

Rob nods. "That spider, I bet he doesn't need feeding every day. Maybe once a week. But unless those kids are huddled in their cave, they're easy pickings. You saw how he sprang out of the grass earlier today. Nobody heard him coming. He's stealthy. And fast. And most of the kids here couldn't outrun him. Or outfight him. The best they can do is try to buy him off with slugs."

The magenta sky switches to black. We huddle around the corner, away from the tunnel's opening. A low grunt echoes up the tunnel. We can hear the big worm, or whatever it is, oozing through it.

"You know," Rob says, "the spider has a name. We should really give the worm a name too."

Steffi grins. "Wormy maybe?"

"Ugh, no. Nothing cute. Something cool."

43

We don't have much else to do, so we debate and agree on Goliath. The name fits his massive size.

Pooky's piercing wails echo down the beach. We curl up on the soft purple grass, confident he can't get into our tunnel, and ignore his screams. We'll figure out how to deal with him tomorrow.

<<<>>>

"Can I ask about Mike?" Frank says.

We're both wading in the stream. I'm filling up the pot and he's washing his hair downstream of me so I don't collect dirty water. Now the area is a safe zone, a few of the other kids wallow in the sweet water and clean themselves, free of worry.

I'd rather not discuss Big Mike, but can't say no. I'd sure want to talk about my brother Cody if anybody knew him. Cody isn't on this island. I've interrogated everyone, but nobody remembers him. And since Frank disappeared from our town around the same time as my brother, he'd have known if Cody had been here.

"Ask away," I say.

"Why didn't he come with you?"

I was afraid he'd ask that. "Frank, you know how Mike was, right?"

Frank nods. "A bully. I know. Even when he was little, he was mean. You left him there because of that?"

I nod and tell him our story. I don't leave anything out. Now that we have our canoe (or what's left of it) in a safe zone, I don't see any reason to lie. The canoe won't do anybody any good now anyway.

Frank sighs. "I'm sorry he gave you so much trouble. I wish he were with you though. No matter what he's done, he *is* my brother."

I nod, understanding. Frank drops the subject, so I ask a couple questions of my own.

"How often do kids show up here?"

"Once a month, sometimes less. It depends. But mortality is high here," he says, confirming Rob's suspicions. "Pooky takes quite a toll."

"How'd you manage to live five whole years?"

Frank shakes his head. "I don't know. Pooky's never really singled me out. And once I lost my glasses, well, now I don't leave the cave much. I can hardly see anything, so the other kids have to lead me around. I hate being such a burden. But maybe I'm still alive for a reason."

"What do you think that is?"

He shrugs and splashes water through his hair. "Maybe Pooky doesn't like the smell of me or something. Anyway, I've been here the longest, so everyone treats me like some kind of ancient guru. I'm like the king here." He lets out a bitter laugh. "I can't help them, though. I can't really do much of anything."

The grass rustles. We stop talking. Hairy black legs waver above the purple blades. Pooky peers over the grass, pincers snapping. He screams. His grotesque head disappears, replaced by a fat black glob pushing into the blue sky.

Pooky's rear end. Any security this safe zone might have had disappears as a long spiral of thick, white goo squirts out the giant spider's abdomen.

A web.

The stuff crashes down on the kid behind me. Matt. He screams as the spider's legs pull the tangled, sticky mess slowly towards the shore.

We stand our ground, knowing if we touch the spider's web we'll stick fast. There's nothing we can do but watch.

GOLIATH

Seawater!" I yell. "Rob!"

Most of our kids are in the sea, splashing around, getting breakfast. They don't hear me.

Matt puts up a good fight, although he's losing it. The spider drags him, inch by struggling inch, towards the grass. The pain from that web must be excruciating. Pooky pulls slowly, reeling the squirming, shrieking boy in like a fish on the end of a grotesque line. The kids behind Matt have already bolted back to their shelter, giving him up as sacrifice for their own safety. Frank stands behind me, staring, eyes wide. He can't see much, but he knows something bad is happening.

The stampeding kids catch Steffi's attention. She barrels towards the beach, her knife outstretched in her hands. She doesn't let that knife out of her sight for an instant. She even swims with it, thank God. Rob scrambles towards his axe lying on the shore.

"Seawater!" I yell, and in stupid desperation I grab the struggling kid.

Once, when I was maybe eight, I got stung by a jellyfish while swimming at the beach. The almost electric sensation had shot across my shin, forcing my leg into an intensely painful spasm. This feels like that. I gasp and fight the tears. Web strings stick me fast to Matt. I grit my teeth and think of Steffi, voluntarily going through this pain twice. I dig my heels in the sandy ground and pull.

The grotesque tug-of-war continues as Steffi plows into the stream, knife slashing. The knife has enough seawater clinging to it for Steffi to saw through the sticky stuff.

"Let's get outta here!" she yells as Pooky, realizing his prey has escaped, positions his rear to shoot another strand. I drag the sobbing Matt, who is now so tangled in the stuff his legs won't even work. Steffi scrambles back to the beach. She grabs our pot and fills it with seawater. Pooky's next coil wraps around Frank, who screams in pain and terror. Steffi throws water on it and it melts away. Frank's screams morph into an intense howl.

"You burned him," I gasp, yanking Matt towards the cave.

"Better than the spider eating him for lunch," Steffi says. "Besides, it can't hurt much worse than that web." She throws seawater on the web stuck to me. The web vanishes and the pain disappears.

Steffi grabs Frank's web-free hand and tugs. "C'mon, let's go!"

Pooky screams his frustration, but he stops throwing thread. We pull his victims into the cave. A few kids roll the rock across the entrance. Frank and Matt are both shaking in the corner.

Frank cradles his burned arm. "Your safe zone didn't work," he gasps.

It works. But I had forgot one thing. Back on Mukade Island, the bad kids couldn't enter our glade, but they were able to throw stuff at us. Rocks. Burning spears. The safe zone won't let living things in, but inanimate objects, spider web included, can break the barrier. The stream is no safer from Pooky now than it was before. Neither, for that matter, is this cave. We'll have to keep the rock in place. If we don't,

Pooky can throw his web into the room and reel the kids out one by one.

"Boy do I hate this place," Steve says.

"Is everybody here?" I ask. Now that Pooky has been denied his breakfast, he'll be in a foul mood.

"Rob and Keiko are missing," Steve says.

We move the rock a fraction and peer out the slit. A big black butt blocks our view. Pooky crouches close, waiting. I drop to the floor and stare between the spider's splayed legs. Past them, in the sea, float Rob and Keiko.

"Well, they're safe anyway," Steffi says, helping to roll the rock back in place. "But they won't be happy swimming out there forever. What do we do now?"

Matt whimpers. He's still covered in spider goo. "There's no way to get that stuff off except the seawater," Steffi says.

"He's covered in it," Keiko whispers. "He'll be burned alive if we use seawater."

"He's spasming like nuts now, Keiko," Rob says. "We have to get that stuff off."

Keiko licks her lips, thinking. "Do we even *have* any more seawater?" she whispers.

Steffi nods and hands her a bowl. Keiko dips her hands in the seawater, barely wetting them. She places her palms gently against the strands covering Matt. She grits her teeth as the web disintegrates.

"Ow," she says. "It's not quite enough seawater to totally dull the web's sting, but hopefully I can get all that silk off without burning the poor kid."

"We need to kill that thing," I say, nodding in the direction of Pooky.

Steffi nods. "How?"

I shrug. "He was scared of us earlier, although I don't know why."

Frank still holds his scalded arm. "He wasn't afraid when we were in the stream."

"No, he wasn't." I try to think of what was different when we charged the spider on the beach. I can't.

A thumping noise interrupts my thoughts. Something beats on the wall behind me. The dirt heaves behind my back. I roll out of the way and stare at the wall.

"It's Pooky," one of the girls whispers. "Oh God, it's Pooky coming through the wall."

"Pooky's out front," Steffi says.

"Then it's another one," the girl says. "There's more than one. What are we going to do?"

Spike flutters near the wall, waiting. "I don't think it's another spider," I say.

"Then what?"

The back wall bursts open. Long, white teeth gnaw through, and a huge, slimy head pokes in. Kids scream.

I laugh. "It's Goliath."

The other kids aren't used to this new monster yet, but we are. I have to believe that Goliath is here to do some good. He turns around and begins to move slowly back the way he came. His abdomen rolls around the tunnel and coats the wall, floor, and ceiling in slimy goo. Steffi reaches out and touches it.

"It's hardened already," she says. "Look, Goliath's slime is what makes these tunnels so smooth and hard. The slime acts like glue; it binds the dirt together. See?"

I pick up one of the shallow bowls, the ones I thought looked like plastic, then run my finger against the wall. The wall and bowl have the same texture. "This must be Goliath's slime too," I say, holding up the bowl. "He must occasionally squirt bits of goo into the sand when he's roaming the beach, and they take on this bowl shape."

Spike lands on my shoulder and chirps. I gasp.

"What? What'd he say?" Steffi asks.

"Two things," I say.

Frank stares at the purple bat. "Two? He only chirped once."

"I know, it's weird. But he doesn't have to chirp much to get his message across. Listen. We can fix the canoe with this stuff."

Steve perks up. "What?"

"Goliath's slime. It's like glue, right? We can take the canoe's broken pieces, and he can glue them together. They'll be as good as new."

"Yeah, but we don't have all the pieces," Steffi says. "Pooky dragged away a good bit of the outrigger, remember?"

Frank's eyes gleam. "If we can fix the canoe, we can leave this place. Right?"

I share a look with Steffi and Steve. No. They can't.

"We can't fit everyone on the canoe," Steve says. "It barely fits the eight of us."

Frank's hopeful eyes turn angry. "So you'll fix it and what, leave us here?"

I try to diffuse the situation. "Look, we don't know what's going to happen. We need to focus on fixing the canoe and figuring out a way to get rid of Pooky. Don't everybody get upset right now."

"What's the other thing?" Steffi asks. "The other thing Spike told you?"

I nod, grateful to have a subject changer. "Goliath has connected the cave here with a room further in."

"Will that help us stay clear of Pooky?" the boy with no arm says.

I nod. "There's no way Pooky can throw his web around corners. The tunnel in front will connect to a room around the bend; that place will be safe."

"And dark," the boy says.

"Dark but safe," I say. "Safety is more important right now."

"What about the stream?" Frank asks. "We still need water from the stream. And the orchard. If Pooky can snare us in the stream, the orchard isn't any safer."

Damn, he's right. "You're still gonna have to deal with Pooky when you want food and water, I guess."

Goliath still petrifies most of the kids, so Steffi, the one-armed boy named Aaron, and I follow the tunnel. It leads to a sharp right bend (Pooky can't fling his web around *that*) and into a large room. Much larger than the crowded cave the kids live in now. I can see around well enough with Spike on my shoulder. "Can you guys see anything?" I ask.

"Yeah," Aaron says. "It's dim, but light is coming from somewhere."

I check out the ceiling. Three holes, spaced evenly across the room, pull light in from above. The holes are encased in a thick, glassy substance. Goliath's slime. They're like sky-lights. Light gets through, but the holes are way too small for Pooky to fit in. He couldn't crack that hard goo even if he tried.

Aaron smiles. "Perfect. Where's Goliath? I want to give that slug a big, one-armed hug."

"It gets even better," Steffi calls to us from another passage. "You guys have a bathroom down here!"

The small antechamber has a deep hole in the center and a light shaft above. A clear bit of Goliath goo covers the hole, but the hardened slime is light and easy to pick up and move to one side.

"Why didn't he help us out before?" Aaron says. "Goliath, I mean? All this time he's been here, and we've never seen him. Why?"

I shake my head. "I guess he's helped you in his own way. He created your cave, and he patrols the beach at night when Pooky is at his worst."

Steffi nods. "He's kinda like the bats on Mukade Island. Before Jack showed up, the bats helped us. But Jack is the only one they'll talk to. It wasn't until Jack joined us that we were able to beat the island and escape it."

Aaron turns to me with wide, excited eyes. "So...the bats trust you, and it seems like Goliath trusts you too. Are you gonna get us out of here?"

I don't want to disappoint him. "You can't leave unless you're immune to the seawater," I say. "If we can't figure out how to get you immune, then I'm afraid you're stuck."

Aaron stares at me with his shining black eyes. He reminds me of Steffi way back, when she thought a little too much of my abilities. "You'll find a way. I'm sure of it."

His praise makes me uncomfortable, but I wonder if he's right. If each of these islands has a protector, like Goliath and the bats, and an evil, like the mukade and the spider, then maybe they also contain a way to immunize kids to the seawater. We have to figure out what that way is.

For the first time, all the island kids get to sleep through the night. Nobody has to watch out for Pooky and hold the rock in place. All the kids except Frank lie crashed out on the floor. Frank and I sit and watch them.

"Thank God Keiko was able to get all that web off Matt without burning him any worse," Frank whispers. "The poison in that web did him enough damage."

"Has he come to yet?" I ask.

He shakes his head. "Not yet. I think it might've thrown him into an epileptic seizure. Now he's just passed out."

"You know, it's interesting," I say. "Rob was telling us how everyone on your island has some sort of physical disability that makes it easier for Pooky to catch you. But on our island, everyone was healthy. We had to deal with more physical stuff, like hunger and thorny grass and warring kids. Sometimes a mukade would get a kid. But mostly, they died slow, of starvation or sickness. You guys here, you eat well and you don't have as many horrors. Just the one. But the same number die because you're no match for Pooky."

Frank stares, unseeing, ahead. He touches his burned arm. "Jack, do you think that they're separating us?"

"Who, the aliens?"

Frank looks at me and laughs. "The what?"

"The aliens. Steffi thinks aliens sent us here."

Frank shakes his head and smiles.

"You don't think they're aliens? I mean, look at all this. We're on some other planet. I didn't believe her much when she first told me, but it's gotta be aliens. This can't be Earth."

Frank stares at me. His eyesight might suck, but his gaze is steady. "You think we're on a different planet."

"Yes. Don't you?"

He thinks for a bit. "No," he said. "I think we're on Earth. I don't think we're somewhere else at all."

"Steffi would like to hear this. Why the hell not?"

"It doesn't fit. I mean, the light that blinks on and off. The flat sky. It's all controlled, can't you see that?"

Now, contemplating this stuff isn't really my strong suit. Even Rob can ponder it better than I can. I've spent a hell of a lot more time figuring out how to survive and get off that damned island than I have trying to determine exactly where we are and why we're here. Steffi's explanation, after a while, sounded reasonable to me. Now it doesn't.

"We're in a hologram or something," Frank says. "None of this is real."

"It sure *feels* real."

"I mean, none of it is natural. It's set up, somehow."

"But why? And by who?"

Frank shrugs. "I don't know. We thought maybe it was to weed out the sick ones. But you guys showing up, well, you've shot that theory all to hell. But if it is a hologram...or at least something artificially made...well, then this world has to have an end. A wall or something. A doorway back to reality. The sea can't go on forever, can it?"

Rob and Steffi cut our pondering short. "Hey," Rob says, ducking into the room. "Can Spike give you some light?"

"What for?"

"We want to take a look at the map."

We've been so busy with other things we've forgotten about the map. I pull it out.

"I can't see how it could be accurate," Steffi says. "But we should take a look at it anyway."

We roll it out. I squint but can't make out much. Night has clicked on. The weird blue glow sends a bit of light down Goliath's holes, but I still can't make out much. Spike flutters over my head and grabs some hair.

"That's better," I say. I peer at the map. Complicated squiggles fill it. Goliath has burrowed all through this island. The areas are marked with pictograms.

"Here's Goliath's chamber, where we found the box." I can tell because somebody has drawn a fat slug on the map. I run my finger down one line, and...

"Look." I gasp, even though I know it's too dark for the others to see it. "Here's the new room Goliath made today. There's the bathroom. It's all here on the map. Crazy."

"But who put it on there?" Rob says.

I shrug. "Goliath?"

Rob snorts. "He doesn't have any fingers. He can't hold a pen."

"Maybe the island did it," Frank says.

"You think so?"

I nod. "Maybe he's right. I mean, look at all the crazy stuff we went through on our island. We figured out the bats controlled a lot of what went on, but they didn't put the treasures on that island, I'd bet."

"Yeah, and if bats don't control this island, something has to," Steffi says.

I nod. "Maybe it controls itself. Or maybe it's Goliath. Or a little of both."

"Or Pooky," Rob says.

Spike chirps.

"No," I say, "not Pooky. He's like the mukade. He's here for population control."

Frank makes a face. "What kind of sick demento sets up a prison like this? Why do we need 'population control'? Seems everyone is doomed to die here anyway." He pauses. "I say we kill that thing. If for no other reason, to piss off whoever set this place up."

I've gotta agree with him. "I think you're right. Especially if we want our wood back. We'll *have* to kill it. It's the only way."

ISLAND KIDS

Steffi and I push through the tunnel. Steffi carries her knife and I have Rob's axe. Nobody else wanted to follow us and risk getting lost in the maze of tunnels, but we decide we'd better see what we can find out.

Spike has studied the map and seems pretty confident on which way to go. Steffi grasps my shoulder as I peer into the murky green depths.

"Just like old times," Steffi says. "You and me, exploring tunnels together. Do you think Pooky uses any of these?"

"No," I say, hoping I'm right. "I think he'd have a hard time fitting down here. He'd be at a disadvantage, he couldn't move fast. This is Goliath's territory."

"Thank God for fat worms with pointy teeth," Steffi says. "I sure hope we don't get lost in here. What are we looking for, anyway?"

"We're looking for Pooky."

"I thought you said he wasn't down here."

"He isn't. But one of these tunnels must end up near his lair, wherever it is. See this tunnel here?" I point to the map.

Steffi punches my shoulder. "You know I can't see a damned thing in here."

"Sorry. Anyway, it's got a bunch of webs drawn at the end of it. I bet if we take that tunnel, we'll end up at Pooky's Place."

"And remind me again why we want to do that?"

"If we can find where Pooky lives, maybe we can kill him."

"Or he can kill us." Steffi shudders. "This reminds me too much of the time we took that tunnel to the mukade's lair. You remember *that*."

I grimace. "How could I forget? But two good things came out of it. I got the first mukade bite, and we found the key to the journal. Steffi, I'll bet you anything if there's a secret to how this island works…to how we can immunize these kids against the seawater…Pooky has something to do with it."

Steffi sighs. "Well, if this trek turns out like that one, I guess it'll be worth it. But how the hell are we gonna kill that spider?"

"I don't know. And we won't try today. I just want to figure out where he lives."

We slink up the tunnel. Getting lost in this maze worries me more than running across anything deadly. Spike helps. He chirps when we hit a turn, and I follow his directions.

"I heard what you and Frank were talking about," Steffi says. "He thinks we're still on Earth somewhere."

"And?"

"Maybe he's right. He seems pretty smart and sounds like he's given it a lot of thought. But I still don't get why. Why would they put us away here? And who *are* they?"

I don't know. But simply the thought that we might be closer to home than we think, that gives me hope. Now the trick is to find our way out of this weird world. There *has* to be a way.

The tunnel slopes upwards. "You think we're near that hill?" Steffi asks.

"We must be. Pooky's lair must be right at the top of it."

The tunnel's end is thick with spider webs. Pooky has all but sealed off the exit with his sticky goo. "Well," Steffi says, "that's as far as we go today. Unless we can get Goliath to chew through it, I'm not getting anywhere near that stuff."

"That's good enough," I say. "Now we know there's a way up here."

Steffi frowns. "Yeah. Now we gotta figure out how to kill a spider the size of a bus."

<<<>>>

"Can I ask you something?"

Steffi stares at me and I stop swimming. We're out for an early morning dip. Pooky is nowhere to be seen. I guess all the excitement yesterday tired him out.

"Ask away," I say as I take a big gulp of seawater.

"What are we doing? I mean, I understand wanting to help these kids. But after we leave here, assuming we can fix the canoe, what then?"

"What do *you* think?" I ask.

Steffi shakes her head. "I don't know. I don't think you know either, exactly, but you know something. Whenever anybody brings up the question, you change the subject."

I'm not comfortable with this conversation so I keep quiet.

"When we left Mukade Island," Steffi goes on, "we were just thinking of escaping that place. Now we've been on the sea for a while, well, what happens next? I mean, where are we heading? If we're on a different planet, or if we're trapped in some wacky hologram like Frank thinks, how will sailing around that sea get us out of here?"

I flip on my back and stare at the sky. "You remember the portal theory we had? Kids pop up here, so there must be a way to pop back?"

"Yeah," Steffi says, "but we could've done that on Mukade Island, if we could have figured it out. That kid Steve knew did it. So you can't tell me we left to find a portal. I don't believe it."

I sigh. "You're right. I'm not looking for a portal. I'm beginning to think they don't exist."

"Then how'd that kid vanish into nothing?" Steffi says.

I shrug. "Maybe whoever sent him here pulled him back out."

"But why?"

I take a gulp of water. "I don't know."

"So we're not looking for a portal, and we aren't sailing around looking for some magical door that'll take us home. You aren't looking for a way to escape this place, are you? You're looking for something else."

It's uncanny how well she gets me. How easy it is for her to figure me out.

"I want to go home," I say, "but I don't want to disappear like that kid did and leave without helping anybody else escape. I think there's a way we can free everybody. Every kid trapped all these islands."

"How?"

"I don't know. But I think Spike was sent with us to help us find something...some*body*. He's on one of these islands. He can explain things to us, tell us what's going on. Why we've been sent here. Who controls Earth."

"And you're hoping this...somebody...will tell you how save everyone and somehow overthrow whoever sent us here to boot?"

I nod.

"Jack, we're kids. The best we *can* do is escape. And I think it's pretty rotten of you to drag these kids all over that sea, pretending we're looking for a way home, when really we aren't."

She says this without sounding mad. "Are you with me?" I ask.

"Of course I am. I just don't think we should force everyone else to come along if we aren't trying to leave this place."

I nod. "If we could kill Pooky, we'd get our wood back and this island would be safe. No monsters left, and Goliath is here for protection. This place could be a safe spot to leave everyone."

"Not everyone," Steffi says. "Not me."

I grin, feeling better. I realize now that this problem has worried me more than I thought. I've felt guilty about forcing these kids to sail over treacherous seas when we aren't trying to find a passage home. Now the secret is out. At least to Steffi. And I can count on her to back me up.

"What'll we tell the others?" I say.

"Nothing, unless they ask. For now, let's concentrate on getting rid of Pooky. But I'm glad we talked, Jack. I've wanted to talk about this for a while. And I'm with you, you know that."

She leans close and kisses me, gently, on my lips. Then she pulls back and gives me an embarrassed smile. For the first time since we left Mukade Island, I feel happy. It's been a while since Steffi really smiled.

That smile disappears as quickly as it came. Steffi's eyes fill with terror, and she gasps. I spin around and see it too... an ominous black cloud blanketing the horizon. It moves towards us at an incredible speed.

A black cloud.

My heart leaps up my throat, and I choke on the seawater I accidentally suck down.

Them. The *things*. They've returned to wreak havoc on this island.

We freeze, mesmerized by the approaching cloud. The island kids, who had been searching the shore for slugs to fend off Pooky, bolt towards the nearest web-free tunnel.

"Stop!" Steffi yells. "Don't move!"

Nobody listens to her. We both shout at the top of our lungs. I watch as Aaron grabs Frank's hand and pulls him towards the tunnel.

"The *things* can get in there," Steffi says. "Those kids need to come out here, with us."

"They can't do that," I say. My stomach sinks so fast, I think I might puke. "They aren't immune, Steffi."

She scans the beach. "Where's Rob and the others?"

"There they are." I point. "They're heading this way."

"Hurry up!" Steffi yells.

Our group dives into the sea, paddling hard. They're going to make it.

But the island kids, they're scrambling down the beach and sprinting towards the tunnels. The blood freezes in my veins.

They're all going to die.

LIGHTNING

We saw what that black cloud did on Mukade Island. Anyone who couldn't reach the sea's protection perished. Eaten alive by millions of swarming little monsters. I know the cloud is close. But I have to help these kids. Somehow.

"Are you nuts?" Steffi yells as I scramble to shore. I don't pay any attention. I stroke as fast as I can. Aaron runs up the beach, squinting desperately, searching for any straggling kids.

"What are you waiting for?" he screams. "Hurry *up!*"

"We've gotta stay in the water!" I yell back. "Can't you see the cloud? Those things will eat you alive!"

"What the hell are you talking about?" Aaron staggers to me and grabs my arm with his one hand. "There are no *things* in that cloud. But it'll kill you if you stay out here. It's a lightning cloud."

I whip my head around and stare at the darkening sky. I turn and study the tunnel entrance. Is he right? Is that cloud *not* what I think it is?

"Trust me!" Aaron yells. He pushes me towards the tunnel. "I've seen that cloud before."

I rip away from his grasp and sprint to the sea's edge, yelling at my group, still bobbing in the water. They can't hear me, but they can see my frantic gestures. They're unsure.

So am I. I don't know *who* is right. The sight of that black cloud scares me. It looks exactly like the cloud that engulfed Mukade Island, except...

A flash of lightning pulses into the sea. That's enough. The kids swim for shore.

They paddle fast, but the cloud moves a hell of a lot faster. It eats up the sea, covering it in a rolling black fog, illuminated occasionally by huge bursts of shocking blue lightning.

We race for the tunnel, careen through the entrance, and slam around a bend. The cloud follows us. Lightning slams on the sand, right before Malika, the last in line, can drag herself into the tunnel.

A bolt hits close to the tunnel entrance. Malika screams and falls.

Steve runs back and grabs Malika's arm. "Pull her in!"

Bhasker, his face ashen, grabs the other arm. Malika is out cold. They drag her across the smooth tunnel floor.

"Further in, quick!" Aaron yells.

The lightning pulses through the ceiling and sends shivers racing up my body, standing my hair on end. I feel dizzy, confused. I concentrate on the person ahead of me: Steffi, her red hair frizzing out in a zillion directions. Spike flutters to me and grabs my hair. My mind clears a bit.

The kids behind me are struggling. Slowing down. I can't decide whether I should stop and help or keep moving. Something tells me, maybe it's Spike, that stopping now will be deadly. I keep running. Steve, Bhasker and Malika fall farther and farther behind.

"We're losing them!"

Steffi doesn't slow down. She either can't hear me in her befuddled state or she's to panicked to stop. The bat fluttering next to my head keeps me semi-alert, but if he wasn't here, I couldn't think straight at all.

My legs won't stop and turn around.

My heart races faster and faster the farther I distance myself from the kids behind me. They're going to die, and it'll be all my fault for leaving them. After a while, I can't hear them at all. And right after that, my panic subsides.

I stop and stare up the tunnel.

Spike chirps. We're through the worst of it. We're deep enough now so the lightning can't reach us.

What about the others?

Spike doesn't know. He won't fly back up the tunnel to find out.

I stop and look around as Spike grabs my hair. I recognize where we are. This is Goliath's room, where we found the box. It's a large room. High ceilings. Dry. Goliath sits in its center.

"Have you been to this room before?" I ask Aaron, as soon as I catch my breath.

He nods. "This is where we hide when the lightning comes."

"I thought you never went in the tunnels."

"Only when the lightning hits. Then we'd even risk meeting up with Pooky."

"What about Goliath?" I ask. "He's here, but I thought you guys said you'd never seen him before."

"We always heard the grunts," Frank says, "but until we met Goliath the other day, when never knew *what* made those grunts."

I'm amazed the kids knew how to find their way down here in the pitch blackness. With Spike's help, I can see. The room glows that eerie shade of green, but the others are completely blind down here.

Several passageways enter the room. A scrambling, squelching sound echoes down one tunnel, and a long, hairy leg reaches into the room. Pooky.

Goliath's slithers towards the spider, and the leg disappears. Pooky's piercing scream echoes around the room. Rob and Steffi start to scream too.

"Calm down!" Frank says. "Pooky isn't gonna hurt anybody. Not in here. He's hiding from the lightning, same as us."

"Yeah, he's never tried to hurt us in here before," Aaron says.

"Probably 'cause Goliath is standing guard," I say.

"Wow," Frank said. "I never even realized that. We figured Pooky was too busy protecting himself from the lightning when he was down here. Eating us wasn't on his agenda."

"Maybe this is like a neutral zone," Steffi says. "You know, like when there's a war, and if the enemies are in that area, they don't fight each other."

"If Pooky had his way, it probably wouldn't be," I say. "But Goliath is making sure nothing happens to anybody down here."

"Too bad that evil monster didn't get caught outside in this storm," Rob gasps. "Then our problems would be solved."

A scraping sound echoes from the passage we just left. Steve and Bhasker stumble in.

"Where's Malika?" Sarah asks.

"Who?" Steve mumbles, gazing around the room. His eyes are unfocused. His hair looks burnt. He wobbles on his feet. Bhasker collapses on the floor.

Bhasker is out cold and Steve is so mixed up in the brain he can't answer our questions. All he can do is slump against the wall, a dazed look in his eyes.

"Come on," I say to Steffi.

I grab her hand and yank her back towards the passageway. Spike screams at me, but I don't listen. Malika is up there. Somebody has to get her.

I commend Steffi for bravely following me, but we don't get far. After a few feet, I'm so dizzy I almost faint. A hand grabs me and pulls me back into the room.

"You can't," Frank says. "It stinks, I know, but you can't get back up there until this storm is over."

"But...Malika..."

"Will she be okay?" Steffi whispers.

"No," Frank says, "she won't."

"Dead?" Rob asks, choking.

"Maybe not," Aaron chimes in, "but the lightning does strange stuff to your brain. A direct hit will kill you."

I shudder. "Malika was awful close to the entrance when that bolt hit the beach."

Aaron nods. "It might have killed her. If it didn't, lying in that tunnel will either do her in or mess her up so badly she won't be good for much."

I'm glad Bhasker is still passed out and can't hear this. He and Malika are tight. This will kill him.

I sit against the wall next to Steve. The other kids have fallen to the floor, tired and spent. Everyone is nervous at the thought of Pooky crouching on the other side of the room, but Goliath positions himself between us. We're safe.

But Malika isn't.

Keiko cries and leans against Rob who has tears streaming down his cheeks. Sarah sits with a blank expression. She's seen worse and unfortunately is way too used to this sort of thing. Steve still slumps forward, eyes unfocused. The island kids huddle together in the middle of the room. We can hear the lightning, but the earth above us muffles the sound.

"How long does this usually take?" I ask.

"Hours," Frank says. "The best we can do is sleep through it."

Nobody shuts their eyes. We may be sitting or lying down, but everyone is tense, alert.

"How often does this happen?" I ask.

"Every couple of weeks," Frank says.

"Every couple of *weeks*?" Steffi whispers to me. "We never had anything like this on Mukade Island."

"Maybe each island has its own natural disaster," I say. "A disaster that never reaches the other islands."

Steffi nods. "Mukade Island has the black cloud with the living things. Maybe that cloud only ever comes to that island."

"But that cloud happens once every twenty years or so. This cloud here comes ever couple of *weeks.*"

"Well," Steffi says, "Maybe the black cloud with the things in it comes so infrequently because it kills off everything when it does. There's no way to escape it, unless you can swim in the sea. Before us, no kid knew how. So, when the cloud came, all the kids would die. It was like the island's way of starting over. But here, instead of a cloud that wipes out everything, they have a cloud that *could* kill you, if you don't get down in the tunnels in time. Your chances of escaping this cloud are a lot greater. So the cloud comes more often."

I nod. "Population control, just another way."

Steve comes slowly around. He is despondent over Malika but won't risk going back after her. "It's a good thing Bhasker's out cold," he says. "He couldn't take this."

"He'll have to take it sooner or later," I say.

"Unless he doesn't wake up," Frank says.

"Is that a possibility?"

"Anything's a possibility. He got enough lightning through his system to pass out. That's never good. But he made it here on his own volition before he fainted. So he might be okay."

"And if he isn't?" Keiko asks. "What will he be like when he wakes up?"

Frank sighs. "I've only had one experience with this. Fortunately, all the other kids the lightning got died."

"Fortunately?" Rob says.

"Yes, fortunately. The one kid who didn't die, he lived in some kind of nightmare. His name was Ramon. He was from Mexico, I think. I could never understand him because all he spoke was Spanish, but after the lightning got him, he never spoke again except in mumbles. He would scream suddenly when you least expected it, get all shaky, and pass out. Even when he was walking around, he was in some sort of trance. A nightmare trance. It was horrible to watch."

"What happened to him?" I say.

"He lived for a bit. Someone always had to watch him because he'd wander off if you didn't. He went right into the tall grass once, before we could haul him back. When the next lightning hit, he had wandered off and didn't make it into the tunnel. We figured that was it for him. But when we came out after that storm, he was sitting on the beach, still alive. Except he still had scrambled eggs for brains."

"It didn't kill him, staying outside in the lightning?" I say.

"Immune," Steffi whispers. "He got immune."

"Yeah, but in a pretty sucky way," I say. "What's the good of being immune if your brain is fried?"

She frowns. "I wonder if he could swim in the sea."

Frank shrugs. "We'll never know. Pooky got him the next morning."

Keiko, who has been listening to the conversation, says, "So Malika..."

"If Malika lives, I'd feel sorry for her," Frank says. "I hate to say it, but I would. She'd be better off dead. Bhasker too, from the looks of it."

We stop talking. I don't want to hear any more and I don't think anyone else does either. We wait out the storm in miserable silence.

<<<>>>

We bury Malika in the tunnel, where Pooky can't dig her up. Everyone cries except Bhasker, who shakes and stares around, eyes unfocused. He doesn't see her. Or us.

Keiko brushes Bhasker's face with one fingertip. "He's lost too."

"Is there anything you can do for him, Keiko?" Rob whispers.

A spark of hope ignites in my heart. If anybody can find a way to fix him, Keiko can.

68

She bites her lip, thinking. "Maybe the seawater will cure him."

Of course. The seawater. Keiko leads Bhasker to the water's edge. He follows like a small child holding a parent's hand. But as soon as his feet touches the lapping water he screams and falls back on the sand.

Angry welts cover his feet.

"It burned him," I whisper. "It *burned* him."

"He isn't immune anymore," Keiko says.

Steve begins to shake. "What about me? I was with Bhasker. I didn't get it as bad as him, but I wonder..."

"Try," I say.

Steve takes a step forward, then hesitates.

"What if..." he starts, staring at the orange waves, fear in his eyes.

"Here," Steffi says. She sticks her hand into the sea and lets a tiny drop fall from her fingertip to Steve's palm. A small, red blister forms on his skin. We stare at it in horror.

"Oh God," Steve moans.

"You're okay though?" I ask Steffi.

"I seem to be," she says, "even though I got some of the lightning too."

I poke my toe into the water. It doesn't burn me. "I'm okay, too. Steve and Bhasker were exposed to the lightning longer, though."

"What will I do?" Steve whispers.

"I don't get it," Steffi says. "Why would getting exposed to lightning reverse your immunity to the seawater?"

I stare out to sea. "Maybe the lightning switches your condition. Maybe if you were one way once, it flips you the other way."

Steve crumples to the ground, sobbing.

I can't think of anything to say to him. He and Bhasker are screwed. They'll never get off this island now.

THE RIFT

I don't really know any of the island kids except Frank, Matt, and Aaron. I wonder if I've avoided getting to know any of them so I won't be sad if they die.

The girl with the limp, Nadia, must have made friends with Malika because she cries for a while. But she finally shrugs it off, like the others do, as another death claimed by the island. Most of the kids avoid both Bhasker and Steve now, as if what they've got might be contagious.

"It isn't though, right?" I ask Frank.

Frank shakes his head. "No, that's not why they're ignoring your friends. They've given Bhasker up as a goner. He won't last long. He'll be Pooky's next target, guaranteed."

He says it flatly, a simple fact. I like Frank, but that tone chills my bones. He goes on. "And Steve isn't immune to the seawater anymore. They were in awe of him before. Now he's as doomed as they are."

This really irritates me. When we got here, we tried to help these kids out. Now they're treating Bhasker and Steve like complete scum. Nobodies. Not even human. I don't get it. Except for Frank, not one of them has said "thank you" for what we've done. They act like they despise us somehow.

As Bhasker continues to shake and stare at nothing and Steve sinks deeper into depression, the island kids distance themselves further. Except for Frank and Matt, who act as go-betweens for the two camps, we don't interact with them much. Our days fall into a dull routine. We swim in the morning, bring fish and seaweed back for Steve and Bhasker, and hole up most of the day to avoid the wandering Pooky. Frank and Matt bring us fruit and water, now that Steve and Bhasker can't drink the seawater, but that's all the interaction we have.

"If those kids refuse to thank us, why should we bother?" Steffi says to Frank one day.

Frank shrugs. "I don't quite know what's going on, Steffi. The other kids...well...they almost seem resentful of your presence here. Like you're bad luck, or something?"

Steffi stares at him, fuming. "How so? They have a better place to live because of us."

"Well..." Frank says, "...that's not exactly what they think. I mean, the worm has always been here. Aaron says that it probably would've made us new digs whether you all showed up or not."

Steffi rubs her chin. "And do you believe that?"

"No," Frank says. "I don't. It seems too coincidental that you would show up in that boat, and suddenly Goliath starts helping us. I think you're the reason why he helped us. But I can't convince some of the others of that. They're getting restless."

Frank sits outside our tunnel entrance, his dull eyes focused on the lapping waves. Steffi, Keiko, and I, sit in the sand next to him. Bhasker and Steve are holed up in the tunnel, and Sarah and Rob are splashing in the sea. It's midday, the part of the day where Pooky is least active. We watch a couple of the island kids wander down the beach, searching half-heartedly for slugs. Aaron, the kid with one arm, catches us staring and shoots us an almost contemptuous look before he turns away. The kids head farther down the beach, toward where we left the canoe.

They've seen the canoe, of course, but can't reach it. Spike had been smart. Some safe zones he made especially for us. The area around the canoe. Our tunnel. The kids can roam anywhere else, but they're forbidden in these two places. And it's starting to piss them off.

"They want it," Frank says, reading my thoughts.

"They're delusional," Steffi says. "What could they do with the canoe? They aren't immune to the seawater, they can't use it on the sea like we can."

Frank shakes his head. "It doesn't matter. You're right, something's changed in their brains. Not all of 'em. But some. They're seeing you as the enemy. And they want off this island before you can take that canoe and sail away."

"We want off this island too," I say, and drop my voice. "But Steve can't go. Or Bhasker. Not in the state he's in."

Steffi nods. "Steve could never survive out on the sea. Even if it didn't burn him to a crisp, we don't have any food for him. I mean, I guess we could take some fruit, but how long will that last?"

"He knows it too," Keiko says. "Why do you think he's so sad? He's stuck."

"Are they all against us then...the island kids?" I ask Frank.

"Well, I'm not," Frank says. "Neither is Matt. Aaron is the main instigator, and a couple of the others agree. Then you have kids like Nadia who are too easily bullied to argue."

Steffi sighs. "We need to figure out how to get Steve and Bhasker better. And we need our outrigger back, or nobody's taking that canoe far. We need to get rid of Pooky. We have to think of a plan."

"If we could figure out why he ran from us that one day," I say. "You know, the day he almost nabbed Nadia. If we could figure it out, we could use it."

Frank nods. "Yeah. Although if he always runs from us, we'll have a hard time catching up with him and killing him."

<<<>>>

Things are pretty dismal in our little tunnel. Bhasker won't eat unless Keiko puts the food in his mouth and even then, he spits most of it out. After a week of shaking and spitting, he's lost several pounds. Steve nibbles at his food, but he's depressed. Really depressed. He sits most days with his back to the wall and stares at the sea. He knows he's stuck here. Helpless.

I don't wish it on him. But in a way, this makes my decision easier. I don't want to take everyone with me when I leave. At the same time, I don't want to leave them stranded. But after what we've been through, I'm betting that each island we reach will have its own perils that we'll have to figure out. The others will be safer if they stay here. There's plenty of food and water. We just need to deal with the Pooky Problem.

Keiko sighs and stares at Bhasker. "I wish there was something I could do for him."

"It's too bad there wasn't anything in that trunk," Rob says. "You know, like on Mukade Island, when we found the vial with the black stuff in it."

The trunk here only contained four things. The axe. The bells. The map. The shield. They're propped in the corner now. We have no idea what the bells are for, or the shield.

Except...

I turn to Rob. "Hey, did you have that shield the day Pooky ran from us?"

Rob stares at it. "No...I don't think so."

"But I did," Sarah says. "It was so damn bulky, I never thought to carry it again. You think *that's* what Pooky was afraid of?"

I shrug. "I don't know, but it's the only thing different that we had that day."

Rob sits up, excited. "Yeah...I mean, what else would you need a shield on a deserted island for, except to shield you from the enemy? It makes sense."

"We had the shield that first day too, though," Steffi says. "When Pooky cornered us in our tunnel."

"It wasn't really near him then though, was it?" Rob says. "I mean, we ran to the back of the tunnel as soon as we heard him scream. Maybe it was too far away to scare him."

"How will we test this theory?" Steffi says. "If that shield scares him, we oughtta use it. But we should test it first."

I nod. "We need to lure Pooky into the open."

Rob shudders. "Is that really a smart idea? What if the shield doesn't work?"

"Don't do it," Steve says.

I turn my head towards him. He hasn't joined our conversations lately, and I'm a bit surprised. Steve's dull eyes stare at me with an intensity and purpose I haven't seen for a while now.

"Don't lure him in the open. That's stupid. He'll eat you for lunch."

"What do you suggest then?" I'd be offended he called me stupid, except I don't like my idea much either. I'm just happy he's interacting with us.

"Wait until the next lightning cloud," Steve says.

Steffi shakes her head. "We don't know when that'll be."

"Frank said it happens every couple of weeks. It's been a week already since the last storm, so in a few days it'll happen again."

"And then what?" Rob says.

"And then, when everyone heads for the cavern, including Pooky, you can try it out."

Boy, am I glad Steve decided to enter the conversation. "He's right. Pooky would've crawled right into the room if it hadn't been for Goliath. All we have to do is approach his tunnel holding up the shield and see if he retreats from it."

"And if he does?" Sarah asks. "What do we do then?"

"We use that shield to get into the island's interior," Steffi says. "And find a way to kill Pooky."

Rob nods. "And get our wood back."

<<<>>>

During the next week, the rift grows deeper between our two camps.

Matt wanders over to our tunnel one day. He can't enter, but Steffi and I step outside to meet him. He tells us his bunch is getting restless. Restless to the point of mutiny.

"I don't get it," he says. "I don't understand what's changed. It's like, ever since that last lightning storm, we've grown divided. But that's never happened before. We banded together. We were scared together. Scared of Pooky, scared of the sea. Scared of the lightning storm too. Now, for some reason, they aren't so scared anymore. And it's making some of them bold."

"Bold in what way?" Steffi asks.

"In a bad way. I mean, it doesn't seem to be happening to everyone. Frank doesn't agree with them and keeps trying to argue with Aaron that he's being unreasonable. A couple of the other kids are okay too, they aren't mean by nature. But there's a few kids, Aaron is the worst, who are beginning to show a bad side. They needed the group to survive, you see. We depended upon each other. Now, they're grumbling."

"About what?"

"About having to take care of the weaker ones. Like Frank. He can't do much because his eyesight is so bad, but before, the kids looked up to him because he was the oldest. The most experienced. But now...it's like they resent him. Some say they should strengthen their position by ditching the weaker ones."

"They wouldn't," Steffi says.

"They would," Matt says. "I've heard 'em discuss it. And fights are starting to break out between the kids. Aaron starts most of 'em."

"Which one is he?" Steffi says.

"The kid with the missing arm," I say. "You know who he reminds me of? Little Mike. Groveling when he needed something, but if he ever got to stab you in the back for his own benefit, he'd take it like a shot."

Steffi and I look at each other.

"The Others," Steffi says.

Matt frowns. "What?"

"On our island, Mukade Island, we called the bad kids The Others. Frank's brother was their leader. They were segregated from us years ago. I think the bats did it for our protection."

"We've never had any segregation here," Matt says. 'We've never needed it."

"You might need it now," Steffi says.

Matt sighs. "Frank's trying, but he's worried that he can't keep the peace much longer. Aaron and some other kids... they want off this island. They want your boat."

"Like they'd last long out there," I say.

"They won't get our boat," Steffi says. "It's in a safe zone. Spike protected it."

Matt nods his head towards the small purple ball of fuzz fluttering above my head. "They want the bat too."

Of course they do. But they can't steal Spike. He won't do for them what he does for us. They can't understand him, for one thing. Only I can. And Spike knows where his loyalties lie. They lie with us.

Matt knows the whole idea is preposterous. But that won't change the outcome. Those kids will revolt at some point. And when they do, we'd better be ready for it.

"It's too bad you can't divide the island," I say to Spike. "Like our island was divided. Each group had its own side."

Spike chirps. I stroke his fur. He has grown in the last couple of weeks, in both size and mind. He's not the same blundering baby bat who started out with us. He's wiser now. More thoughtful and less fluttery. More in charge. I bet he can divide this island if he wants to. But that's the trick. He has to want to. I can ask him to do something, but that doesn't mean he'll do it.

"If it comes down to sides," I say, "which will you pick?"

Matt frowns, thinking. "They're my friends," he says. "But if it comes down to fighting, I won't be on Aaron's side."

"How many kids do you think *will* be on his side?" Sarah asks.

Matt shrugs. "Five or six, I'd bet."

Steve sticks his head out of the tunnel. "What's going on?"

"Nothing, except Matt thinks some of his kids are gonna try to ambush us and take the boat," Steffi says.

Steve shakes his head and sighs. "They can't live out on that sea. No more than I can."

"So now we have to deal with Pooky *and* mutinous kids," Steffi says.

I nod. And I have a feeling we'll deal with them all in one place. In the tunnels. During the next lightning storm.

THE CHASE

It happens a couple days later. We cower in Goliath's room and listen to the muffled lightning cracks outside.

Bhasker shakes in the corner. Steve sprawls next to him and stares into the blackness. He can't see anything but he can hear the distant booms and the closer scrapings of Pooky, huddled in his tunnel. Goliath squishes and grunts in the room's center.

The kids are quiet, grouped together in clumps. Our bunch is farther in this time; the island kids are closer to the tunnel's entrance. Frank and Matt sit between the groups like human shields. I sit with my back propped to a wall and shiver. The cavern is much colder than the warm beach.

In the swirling confusion of escaping the deadly lightning cloud, we almost forgot to grab the shield. I swiped it up at the last minute before I ran down the tunnel. Steffi has her knife, like always, and Rob carries the axe. We're armed. We're ready.

We had discussed at length our plan of action. Steffi was all for driving Pooky backwards as far as we could. Her hope was that we'd push the spider so far up the tunnel that the lightning effects would do him in. I don't think that's likely. We'll have to push him back pretty far, and we'll probably succumb to the effects before Pooky will. And I refuse to end up like Bhasker or Steve: at worst practically comatose and rambling, at best no longer immune to the seawater.

"If we could wait until after the lightning was over," Rob had said, "we could push him *all* the way back up the tunnel maybe."

I nodded. "We could."

"Yeah, as long as the storm ends well before dark," Steffi said. "I don't want to get stuck in the middle of the island in the dark. You can bet Pooky has his hideout covered with sticky webs, and I don't want to stumble into one."

"We'll have to watch out for the flinging webs too," Rob said. "We don't want him snaring us for dinner."

We agreed to wait until the storm was over and then try pushing Pooky up the tunnel. That is, of course, if the shield actually works.

As we huddle in the chilly cavern, my heartbeat intensifies. The idea seemed solid enough when we were walking along the warm beach. Now, I'm beginning to question the idiocy of this plan. I suppose if the shield doesn't work, the worst thing that'll happen is nothing, it just won't work. Goliath will protect us while we're in the cavern; we don't have to worry that Pooky'll grab us for a mid-lightning storm snack.

But if it *does* work, will we have the guts to follow through with this crazy plan? The shield might not kill Pooky, but it could protect us enough to at least explore the island's interior. We may even luck out and get our wood back. But this whole expedition could end in disaster. Ugly disaster involving spider jaws and tangled webs.

"I wish we had some seawater with us," Steffi says. "We could use it to dissolve any webs in our way."

We hadn't had the time or foresight to grab a bowl of it and take it with us. We were running for our lives as soon as the black cloud appeared over the horizon.

We sit in tense silence. The island kids are a little more relaxed. They're used to this sort of thing, and their plan is to wait it out and return to their tunnel.

I *think* that's their plan.

I scoot over to Frank and Matt.

"What's going on?" I whisper.

"What?" Frank answers. "Nothing, why?"

"You two are sitting between everyone, like referees. Are you worried your kids might do something?"

I glance over at the other kids. They're straining to hear us, so I keep my voice down to a barely audible whisper.

"They're planning on rushing you for the knife and axe," Matt murmurs. "I overheard Aaron and some of the other kids talking about it."

"Thanks."

I scoot back to my group. "We have a problem. The other kids, they want the knife and axe."

"Crap," Steffi says.

I'm worried about something else, as well. There's ten of them and seven of us. Six, if you don't count Bhasker, who wouldn't be any use in a fight. The original plan was for me, Steffi, Rob, and Sarah to deal with the spider. Steve and Keiko would take Bhasker back to our safe zone.

Problem is, we didn't bring the spear, so Steve has no protection. If the kids are after our weapons then maybe they won't bother with Steve and Keiko, but I can't be sure. What if they try to capture them for hostages or something?

"I'll stay with them," Sarah whispers. "As soon as the lightning stops, we'll head back up the tunnel."

"The other kids are blocking the tunnel," Rob says.

"Damn, that's right. What about one of the other tunnels?"

"Take that one behind you," Steffi whispers. "I've been studying the map. I'm pretty sure that one is the tunnel we took the first night we landed. It'll put you on the other side of the island, and you'll have to hope the exit isn't covered with Pooky's webs, but I think that's Goliath's main exit and he keeps it fairly web-free. And if the other kids get too close to you, you can always escape to the sea."

"No," Steve says, "we can't."

"Oh crap, I forgot. Sorry, Steve. But that tunnel is the only chance you've got. The island kids could follow you, of course, but you'll have the advantage. They don't know where that tunnel goes. It has some bends in it; you'll have to be careful, but once you get to the beach, at the worst you can hide out in the safe zone where we've stashed the canoe."

"Yeah, you can duck under it," Rob says. "Even Pooky's webs couldn't hurt you there."

"You'll have to make a dash for it," I say.

I tell Frank and Matt our strategy. I figure if they were willing to rat out the island kid's plans, they're on our side, not theirs.

"I'd like to come with your group," Frank says to me.

"Into Pooky's lair?"

"If it can be done, yes. Matt, will you help Jack's friends if our kids decide to attack?"

"I will," Matt says. "I'll try anyway."

We can tell the lightning is abating. The tremors are fewer and further between. Goliath shifts restlessly in his slime. He knows we're planning something, I'm not sure how. Maybe Spike told him.

"Now," I whisper to the others. "Let's do it now. If we're quiet, they won't even realize we're doing anything since they can't see us."

"How do we know where we're going?" Frank asks.

"Elephant-train it," I say. "I'll go first, I can see. Plus, I've got the shield. Steffi, hold on to me, Frank to Steffi, Rob to Frank."

"Why do I have to go last?" Rob whines.

"Because you're the biggest. And Frank can't see."

81

"I can't see either, not in this blackness."

"Geez, Rob, grow a little backbone and protect us from behind. You've got the axe."

"Oh yeah," Rob says. "I forgot about that."

We creep as silent as we can towards Pooky's hole. Goliath grunts but doesn't try to stop us. In the dim light I can see Pooky's hairy legs grouped in a disgusting heap, all ten of them. I raise the shield as we approach.

The spider moves backwards.

Scrambles is more like it. He doesn't screech, thank God, so the island kids still don't suspect anything.

I take a step into Pooky's tunnel.

The air is thick here. Thick with fear from us and an even more urgent fear from the great spider that inches away from the shield, farther and farther up the passageway. Elation fills my chest and pushes some of my fear away.

"It's working," I whisper.

"Keep going," Steffi says. "Boy am I glad I can't see that thing."

We move slowly up the tunnel. I hear a shout, and freeze.

"It's okay," Frank says. "Well, at least I hope it is. Your bunch must've run down the back tunnel. I think my kids are following them."

"I hope they get back okay," Steffi mutters. "I wish we had left them something to defend themselves with."

"That's what Aaron's group were after though," Frank says. "It's better you have the weapons with you. They aren't going to follow you up here. They think we went up that other tunnel, and they won't realize their mistake until too late."

Nevertheless, we move faster, confident now that Pooky will continue to retreat before us.

I hear a grunt and glance behind me. Goliath blocks the tunnel behind us. Even if the island kids *did* try to follow us, they couldn't push past his blubbery behind.

When the tunnel widens, the spider shifts around, legs scrambling along the walls, Steffi, hearing the ruckus, grips my shoulder so tight I'm surprised my collar bone doesn't shatter into a million pieces.

"Careful," I hiss.

"What's he doing?"

"Running away. Wait, here it comes."

A long white string of stickiness shoots out of Pooky's behind, smacks into the shield, and shatters. Literally *shatters*. Like it's turned to ice. I watch it fall and break. Keeping one eye on Pooky and my shield high, I reach down and touch a piece.

"It isn't sticky. Or painful."

"What isn't?" Steffi whispers.

"The web Pooky flung at us. It hit the shield and solidified." I pass the piece backwards. It feels light, like it's turned to plastic.

Pooky realizes his webs won't do any good with the shield up, and he bolts for the entrance. We follow him until we reach the tunnel's end. Light streams into the entrance, but a thick web blocks our advance.

"He did that in a hurry," Steffi says.

I move to the web and tap the shield against it. It falls, a huge, round, sphere. Solid.

"Wow," Rob breathes.

"Let's go," Steffi says, pushing past me.

"No, wait!" I yell after her. She stops.

"Look, this shield works as long as we can block Pooky's web with it," I say. "But if he's out there, crouching over the tunnel, and shoots his web on us from behind, the shield isn't going to do as much good. Let me go first. He's scared to get anywhere near the shield. Unless his web hits me, I'll be safe. Stay here a second."

They agree. I don't much care for being the first person out, but I don't see any option. I have no idea how far Pooky will distance himself from the shield. It could be yards, it could be mere feet.

I mean to creep out slowly, but at the last second I freak out and make a dash for it, spinning around wildly, hoping to catch Pooky before he catches me.

He's disappeared. I don't see one hairy leg.

"Come on out," I say.

For the first time in the weeks we've been here, I don't see the sea. It's out there, I can hear it, but the tall purple grass obliterates it from view. Several trails span away from the tunnel opening, but I can't see where they go.

"I don't like this grass," Steffi says. "That spider could be anywhere."

We're safe in our little clearing, but I agree with her. The thought of searching those trails is daunting.

"What should we do now?" Rob says.

Frank peers around, squinting. "We're dead-center, I bet. Everything slopes down from here, what little slope there is. This is the highest point on the island."

"That spider has to make *some* noise," I say. "He's got to be somewhere."

"Why don't you ask Spike to look for him?" Rob says.

Spike flutters above my head and stares around with interest. "Spike, see if you spot him. But fly up high so he can't fling a web at you."

He chirps, soars in the air, and returns in a couple of minutes.

I listen to his chirps. "Pooky is at the pond."

Frank's eyes widen. "The *pond?*"

"That's what Spike says. Must be a pond down this path. Pooky isn't lying in wait for us, according to Spike. He's curled up in his nest."

"Where our wood is, I'll bet." Steffi says.

I step forward. "Let's go check the pond out."

"Wait," Rob says. I can tell a whine is imminent. Rob wants to be brave, but he fails a heck of a lot more than he succeeds.

"Do you want to go back?"

"Seems like a better idea than heading right to where we know that monster is, shield or not," Rob says.

"Well, he's far enough ahead of us now, and there's Goliath waiting in the tunnel," I say. "If you can push past his slimy body, you'll probably be safe."

Rob realizes nobody else is going to back down. He steels himself. "No, I'll go."

Spike flies high and keeps guard. He'll let us know if he spots Pooky.

I take a deep breath and plunge down the winding path.

THE POND

I don't like this," Rob says. "It's too creepy. I can't see anything through this grass."

"It's like being on a whole different planet," Frank says. "I mean, all this time we could see the meadow but never could explore it.

"Why not?"

"What do you mean, 'why not'? This is Pooky's territory. Kids who disappear in the grass disappear for good. It isn't worth tromping through. Plus, this island is so small, we figured all we'd find would be grass and a big spider's nest. Spike really said *pond*?"

"He did."

"He could've told us about it before," Steffi grumbles. "You know that bat has flown all over this island. He must've known about the pond days ago."

"Yeah, but he wasn't ready to tell us until now," I say.

"Why not?"

I shrug. "I don't know, Steffi. The bats pick and choose the information they want to give us. It's almost like they want us to figure out as much as we can before they fill us in on the rest." I push some long purple grass blades out of the way. "Anyway, if there's a pond, the stream below must flow from it."

"I wonder where the pond water comes from," Steffi says.

"Well," Frank says, "it never rains here, except when the lightning storm comes. Then it dumps buckets. Maybe the lightning rain fills the pond."

"I can't believe Pooky is so scared of that shield he won't try anything," Rob says. "Why is he so afraid of it?"

"You saw what it did to his web," Steffi says. "Maybe it does the same to him. Maybe if the shield touches him, he shatters."

"That'd be an easy way to kill him off," Rob says. "If you can get close to him with that thing."

"I doubt it," I say. "No way can I run as fast as something with ten legs."

"Hold up," Rob says. I turn around; he's stopped moving and has lowered his axe. "So what are we doing here then, if we aren't gonna kill Pooky?"

"Well, if we can scare Pooky from his nest, we can grab the piece of outrigger we're missing."

He frowns. "And do what with it? How're we going to reattach it?"

"Goliath's sticky goo," Steffi says. "Goliath can fix the piece, remember?"

Rob nods and picks up his axe. We continue our slow creep down the path. Every so often I have to break a strand of web with the shield. Pooky has scattered his threads along the track. It's a pain-in-the-ass deterrent.

"You think Pooky knew that there was a box with a shield in it? Something that could do him in if the kids found it?" Rob says.

Steffi laughs. "He's a spider, Rob. He can't think."

"I dunno. He seems pretty smart to me."

The trail ends in a clearing. I stop and suck in my breath.

"Holy cow, would you look at that," Rob says.

Frank gulps. "Wow."

The pond shimmers in the afternoon sun. Crystal clear, it lies on a bed of silvery sand. Small, blue dots shine in the water, giving the whole pond an eerie but beautiful glow.

A huge nest of grass, web, and white things lines the pond's far bank.

"Bones," Rob says grimly, squinting at the white things.

"Oh, gross," Steffi says, making a face.

I shudder, wondering how many kids over the years Pooky has captured to make that horrible nest.

"I see the outrigger," Rob says. "Right on the edge, if we can get to it."

A long black leg pokes out of the nest, waves in the air, and curls around the wood, as if the spider senses what we're after.

"Well, at least we can see him," Steffi says. "I'd rather not, he freaks me out, but if we see him, we know where he is."

"He isn't going to risk getting anywhere near this shield," I say. "Not if your theory is right and he shatters if he touches it."

"I wonder what those blue glowing things in the water are," Rob says.

"You think that's what makes the island glow at night?" Steffi says.

I nod. "Must be."

Rob peers over the pond's edge. "What are they?"

I move to the bank. The blue dots float around, pulsing light and wiggling. They're each the size of a grain of rice.

"Spike, is this safe?"

Spike chirps. I stick my finger in the water. The blue specks congregate to my finger in an instant, covering it. They tingle against my skin.

"Maybe that isn't such a good idea," Steffi says. "You don't know what those things will do."

"No, Spike says it's okay."

I pull my finger out of the water. The blue things let go.

"What'd it feel like?" Rob asks.

"Neat," I say, "Vibrating, like a massage."

"Can we swim in there?" Rob asks Spike.

The bat chirps. "We can," I say, "but we'll have to leave the shield on the shore. Water can mess it up."

"What do you mean?"

I'm not sure exactly, so I shrug. "Spike says the blue things are living cells and they eat away bad things. I don't know what he *means* by bad things. But the water they're swimming in will mess up the shield. It might lose its power against Pooky."

"Well, we don't want *that*," Frank says.

"Will the water mess up us too?" Steffi asks.

I shake my head. "No. For us, the water is just water."

"Someone has to stand guard if we want to get into that water, then," Rob says.

"I don't think we should go in," Frank says. "Not now. We didn't come up here to play. We came up here to get the wood for your boat, remember?"

Rob nods. He remembers. But I don't blame him. Swimming with these cool blue things is a lot more appealing than sifting through a spider's nest full of kid bones.

"I'm surprised the lightning hasn't killed them," Steffi says. "The blue dots. If they're living things, are they immune to it?"

"Maybe," Frank says.

Everything else, meaning Pooky, Goliath and the kids, is forced deep into the caverns when the lightning comes. These little living things seem to thrive in it. And I wonder...

"It's the same kind of light."

Steffi pulls her gaze away from the mesmerizing dots. "What?"

"That light they're giving off. Doesn't it remind you of the lightning? Same color."

Steffi narrows her eyes. "What are you thinking now, Jack?"

My brain races, and an excited tingle runs down my spine. "Listen. I think the lightning doesn't kill these bugs because they *feed* off it. That's how they get their light."

Rob frowns. "So what you're saying is…"

Frank grins. "I'm following you, Jack. If these cells eat lightning, maybe they have the same properties the lightning does…but in a more positive way. Instead of killing you like the lightning will, they help you instead."

"They eat away 'bad things'," I say. "Maybe it'd be a good idea to bring Bhasker and Steve up here."

"For what?" Rob asks. He dangles his finger in the water so the blue things will tackle it.

"Maybe if they drink it, it'll cure them so they can swim in the seawater again."

Steffi nods in agreement. "Couldn't hurt."

Rob yanks his finger back. "Yeah, but if these bugs work the same way the lightning does, wouldn't that mean we'll *lose* our ability to swim in the sea if *we* drink it? 'Cause that's what the lightning did."

I listen to Spike's insistent coos. "I don't think so. I think these things take the lightning and make it work for the best. This pond is how the kids from this island can get immune to seawater."

"If only we'd known there was something up here," Frank whispers.

"Yeah, but you'd never have guessed it. Pooky is here to protect it. It's like on Mukade Island: there's a way to find the island's secrets and beat them, but there's always something guarding those secrets. The mukade guarded the secret on our island. Pooky guards it here."

"Do you think maybe if we drink this water we'll become immune to Pooky?" Steffi says. "Like how the seawater made the mukade fear us?"

I shrug. "Who knows? But I'll bet anything that if Frank drinks this water, he can swim in the sea."

"I'm going to try it," Frank says. He scoops his hand in the water. The blue things practically jump into his cupped palm. Frank brings the water to his lips and takes a tentative sip.

"Sweet," he says. "This doesn't taste like water at all." He drinks the rest. "You guys should try this."

Rob still looks nervous. "I dunno. I'm already immune to the seawater, I don't know what good it'll do me."

"It can't hurt," I say. "Spike says we should."

The little bat has already dived down and slurped some water himself. I drop to my knees and scoop a handful of the little blue things up to my mouth. They have no texture. I expect a grainy taste when I gulp them down, but the liquid is smooth, with a sweet, sugary, taste. I smack my lips.

"This is nothing like the water that flows into the stream," Steffi says, wiping her mouth with a dripping hand.

Spike flutters closer and gives me gives an insistent chirp. I glance away from the water.

Pooky has climbed out of his nest and sidles around the pond, his multitude of glinty eyes watching us. He's either trying to escape or attack. I laid the shield in the grass while I took that drink. Now I grab it. Pooky hesitates.

"It's been watching us like a hawk," Steffi says. "I bet the second you put down that shield, it started creeping this way. That hideous thing. I can't wait until we get rid of it."

Pooky's warning is enough to remind me why we're here. "Come on," I say.

I hold the shield in front of me and march around the pond. Pooky backpedals towards his nest, but he knows we're heading that way.

"Stay close together," I tell the others.

"Do we have to go near those bones?" Rob says.

"If we want the outrigger back, we do. Let's get this over with and get out of here. We can bring Bhasker and Steve up here tomorrow."

Pooky screams at us but retreats into the grass. I thrust the shield at Rob. "Take this and guard us. We'll get the outrigger."

Rob's shaking hand grabs the shield. "Okay. But hurry up."

White sticky strings drape over the outrigger like a sinister veil, but the shield quickly dispatches that problem. The outrigger is light in relation to its size. Spike resumes his position high in the sky, and we drag the wood to the tunnel where Goliath patiently waits.

"Thanks Spike," I say. "And you too, Goliath."

The great worm gives a short bark and scoots down the tunnel. We follow him, knowing Pooky will never dare challenge both Goliath and the shield. We're safe. And we have the outrigger.

And possibly, we've found help for Bhasker and Steve. And the rest of the kids.

"You think Goliath will help us out with the gluing bit?" Steffi asks.

"I think he will," I say. "At least I hope so."

<<<>>>

When we reach our safe zone, Frank walks right in. Matt is there too. I'm not surprised. Spike has set up the safe zones so kids can pick a side. If a kid wants to harm us, he can't enter. But if he's truly our friend, he can cross the border. That happened on Mukade Island too. When we rescued Little Mike, he could get into our side. But when he turned traitor, the safe zones reversed on him.

Steve isn't as ecstatic about the wood retrieval as I thought he'd be.

"It's fine for all of you," he growls, "but I can't drink the seawater anymore. Even if you get the canoe fixed, I can't go. I might as well be dead."

Steffi grins. "Don't say that yet. Wait until you see the pond."

Steve frowns. "The what?"

92

"The pond. It's where that blue glow comes from. Jack says that Spike says that if you drink the water there, you can swim in the sea again."

Steve grabs my arm. "You think that'll work?"

"There's one way to find out," Frank says. "I took a good swing of that water. Help me down to the sea."

We keep an eye out for both Pooky and the other island kids as we head for the beach. The coast is, literally, clear.

"We've got around twenty minutes before the lights click off for the day," Steffi says. "Let's do this quick."

Frank moves cautiously to the sea's edge. Steffi wades out, cups some water in her palm, and brings it back.

"Hold out your hand."

Frank stares at the water. He stretches a shaking hand towards Steffi's. She pours a little water out of her cupped palm. Frank sucks his breath in and yanks his hand away.

"Damn," Steffi says. "It didn't work?"

Now Frank's eyes are getting larger. His hand inches forward. I don't see a burn on it.

"It works," he says, tears streaming out of his eyes.

"C'mon then," Steffi says, grabbing his hand and pulling him towards the surf.

Frank hesitates, but once his feet hit the water, he gives a whoop and jumps, belly flopping, into the waves. We follow him, laughing. He holds his arm up.

"Look! The burn I got when Steffi splashed the spider web is gone."

Steve watches us from the shore, a grin spreading across his face.

"You think it'll work for me too?" he asks when we finally slosh out of the water and head to the tunnel. "I mean, it worked for Frank, but he's never been changed by the lightning. I'm a little scared. Maybe since the lightning's changed me once, the blue things won't work on me."

"Well, can't hurt to try. We'll get you up to the pond tomorrow, once it's light."

"That's fine," Steve says. "As much as I want to return to normal, I'm with you. Going up to Pooky's hideout at night sounds a little too risky to me."

We move inside as the lights blink out. Frank flops down beside us, happy. Matt grins. "It'll work on me too, right?"

"Don't see why it wouldn't," Steffi says.

Keiko taps Frank's shoulder. "Drink lots of the seawater. Every day. It will make your eyes get better."

Frank gulps. "You think?"

Steve nods. "I had a bad eye once. The seawater fixed it. Keiko's right. The more you're in that seawater, the better your eyesight'll get."

Frank looks like he's about to bolt for the sea again. I bet he'll be in the water more than out of it, after this. He only settles down when we hear Pooky's scream and know he's on the prowl.

Steve sits next to me, chomping on a piece of fruit. "You really think it'll work, Jack? The pond water?"

"I hope so."

"If the seawater worked on Frank," Keiko says softly, "then we can get all the kids immunized. We should let them know."

Steffi shakes her head. "We shouldn't immunize the bad ones."

"We must, Steffi. It isn't fair to make them suffer."

"Keiko's right," Rob says. "Running into the sea is an easier way to escape Pooky than trying for a tunnel. They'll be safer. And maybe, once they're immune, we'll all be friends again."

"Or they'll get worse," Steffi says. "Like The Others. They were pretty bad."

"Not all of 'em," Sarah says, frowning. "I wasn't bad. Neither were Bhasker and Malika."

"Sorry," Steffi says. She doesn't make eye contact with Sarah. They've never been on the friendliest of terms. "But if we immunize them, they'll want to come with us. And we can't fit 'em on the boat."

"What about me and Matt?" Frank says.

Steffi glances at me. I turn away. My stomach is starting to clench, like it used to when I had to take a test I hadn't studied for. I don't even want to take the kids from Mukade Island, let alone new kids, and Steffi knows it. How do I even bring this up to my friends? They'll hate me for it. They'll think I'm a traitor.

BHASKER

I lie awake that night, my stomach refusing to unclench. I run through the options again and again, trying to figure out how to convince everyone to stay on this island and let me go alone. The trouble is, I can't really think of a good reason. The vague but insistent idea that there's someone I have to find, and find alone, sounds flimsy even in my own head.

Bhasker can't go. If the pond water immunizes him and Steve to the seawater again, that's great, but Bhasker's still practically a vegetable and would need too much care. I might convince Keiko to stay with him. She doesn't like the sea anyway; she'd much rather stay on dry land. And if Keiko stays, Rob might. He won't want to leave her.

I want Steffi with me. But is that because my mind is telling me she's essential to the plan, or is it because I like her too much? She's strong and fierce, but to be honest, Sarah is stronger and fiercer and much more level headed. I couldn't take them both: Steffi and Sarah have never been close, although the further along we get, the nicer they've been to each other. But Steffi called Sarah a traitor once, and Sarah's never forgiven her for it. I'd love Sarah's extra muscle. But I don't want any friction on the boat.

96

Sarah should be my first choice, but she isn't. Steffi is. And no matter how I try to convince myself otherwise, the idea of having Steffi with me when I sail away is as insistent as finding this stranger is.

I lie in the darkness, listening to everyone's breathing. They're all expecting freedom from this place once we fix the outrigger. And if we immunize the other kids, they'll be expecting it too. What are my choices? Steal the canoe and slink out of here at night like a thief? Or bring up the subject and hope everyone agrees with my idea to leave them here?

They won't agree to it. *I* wouldn't agree to it, if someone laid it out for me. How can I expect them to?

I finally doze off, but it seems only moments before the lights switch on. Steve is already rousing us, eager to get up to the pond.

"Maybe we should wait until midday," I mumble. "When Pooky is at his sleepiest."

"What does it matter, we've got the shield. C'mon, Jack. I hardly got any sleep last night, I'm so excited to see if this'll work."

My stomach clenches again. I have to broach the subject at some point. But the kids are up and stretching, and Keiko is shaking Bhasker's arm to wake him. Now isn't the time.

Steve, Keiko, Bhasker, Matt, and I head out after we get something to eat. I stay out front with the shield. Steve and Keiko lead Bhasker, who follows, docile and unseeing, and Matt brings up the rear. The others stay behind. We've decided it's better to go to the pond in small groups. That way we can stick together and the shield can protect us all. I'll stand guard with the shield. Spike will fly in the air and tell us where Pooky is.

"It'll be hard when we leave," Steve says, "if the other kids don't have Spike. How will they know where Pooky is lurking then?"

Keiko stops dead in her tracks. "The bells," she whispers.

"What?" Steve says.

"The bells! The bells that are in the trunk. We tried to figure out what they were for, but that's it. We need to put the bells on Pooky. Then we'll always know where he is."

"Isn't it weird," Steve says as we move up the trail, "how each of these islands has, stashed away somewhere—items that you need to survive? It reminds me of that game I played when I was a kid."

"What game was that?" Keiko says.

"I can't remember what it was called, it was-some stupid computer game, but in it, you had to find something to help you move forward. Like you couldn't open a door unless you found the buried key. Or you'd have to collect a sword before you could fight the dragon. You know, that sort of thing. Doesn't it feel like that now? Only in real life?"

"A bizarre real life," I say, "but you're right. The shield keeps Pooky away. The bells, if we can figure out how to attach them, will let everyone know where he is."

"What about the axe?" Keiko says.

Steve shrugs. "A weapon, I guess. Although what you need an axe here for on an island with no trees is beyond me. There's nothing to chop."

"We could've used it on Mukade Island," I say, remembering how long it took us to build the canoe. An axe would have come in handy then.

We reach the pond. Blue dots dance in the water. From his nest, Pooky blinks surprised eyes at us, probably wondering why we're back so soon.

"Well, I'm glad he's here. At least we can keep an eye on him," I say, locking eyes with the spider. "I'll stay here on the bank as guard. You guys take Bhasker in."

Keiko and Steve lead him into the water, Matt following. The blue microbes gravitate to Bhasker, leaving the other three untouched. They cover his body until I can't see anything but his head.

"Dunk him in," I say. "Let them cover him completely."

Steve pushes Bhasker's head under the water. "You sure this is okay?" he asks, staring at the now-blue boy. "You sure they aren't hurting him?"

Bhasker starts to struggle and Steve releases him. Bhasker sits up, spluttering.

"What are you doing? he yells.

Steve breaks into a grin and flings his arm around the boy. "It works!" he says, hugging Bhasker close.

"Get off me," Bhasker says, pushing Steve away. "What's going on? Where are we?"

He looks absolutely petrified, but at least he's talking and making sense. We wait until he calms down, then explain what happened.

"Do you remember anything?" Keiko says.

Bhasker shakes his head. "I remember having a horrible dream. The air was full of those black flying things, you know, like the things that attacked Mukade Island. They kept eating me, over and over, down to the bones. I'd wake up thinking it was a dream, but then they'd come again and it would start all over." He shudders. "I'm glad it was just a dream."

"A long dream," Keiko says, stroking his head. "You were out for two weeks."

We tell him everything that has happened. Including Malika. Bhasker stares at us, looking as uncomprehending as he had a few minutes ago when he was still grappling with his nightmare. Keiko, after taking a few gulps of water, escorts him back to shore. He sinks to the grass, only to bolt up screaming when he notices Pooky staring at us from his bed.

"It's okay," Keiko says. "We're in the island's interior now. Pooky is afraid of the shield. He won't come near us. Coming out Steve?"

"In a minute," Steve says. Now that Bhasker has left, the blue things are clinging to Steve. "Jack, do you really think the blue things will fix our seawater problem?"

"We can sure hope so," I say. "The blue things work for the lightning. Hopefully they'll reverse the seawater curse too."

<<<>>>

Everyone's mood improves drastically, even Bhasker's. He is devastated by Malika's death, but he's seen death before. So have we all. The immunizing process works as well, and now both Steve and Bhasker can enjoy swimming in the sea again.

My mood, meanwhile, disintegrates. We have the outrigger. We have our friends immunized and ready to go. How do I break it to them that I must go alone, with only Steffi to accompany me?

I bob in the waves, eyeing Pooky, who's crouched in the grass watching us swim. A hand touches my shoulder. "What're you thinking, Jack?" Steffi whispers.

"How do I tell them?" I say.

She understands with no further explanation. "Well, once we reattach the outrigger, we could wait until nightfall and take the canoe before anyone notices."

"I thought about that. I can't do it, Steffi. It seems too... sneaky."

"Well then, the only other choice is to sit everyone down and discuss it," she says. "They aren't going to like it."

"Not going to like what?" Matt, who is closest to us, says. His voice is loud enough so the others turn our way.

I steel myself. Now's the time. But as I stare at the others, dripping with seawater and staring confidently...hopefully... at me, I can't do it.

"Jack thinks not everyone should leave the island," Steffi says. "In fact, he's thinking the two of us should go and the rest of you should wait here."

Rob stares at me. "What's she talking about, Jack?"

I take a deep breath. "It could get rough out there. We don't all need to go."

Sarah looks thunderous. "Are you crazy? We've gotta find a way out of this place. A way home."

Rob frowns. "Yeah. Isn't that the plan?"

"No," Steffi says. "At least, that's not what Jack's thinking."

Sarah's eyes are flashing daggers. "So we've been roaming around for nothing? We could've stayed on Mukade Island, if that was the case. We had it better there."

"Here's better, I think," I say. "Except for Pooky."

"It damn well isn't," Sarah says.

Steve puts his hand on her shoulder. "Calm down, Sarah. Jack, I want to know what we're doing sailing around that sea at all if we aren't trying to find a way home."

"We *are* trying to find a way," I say. "There's somebody out there, on one of the islands. I don't know who, I think Pepe must've put the idea into my head back when we were on Mukade Island. Whoever he is, he holds the key to escaping this place. For *everyone* to escape and go home. I have to find that guy."

"And we don't all have to go," Steffi says. "It'll be rough anyway. We don't even know where to look. We could be gone for months. Or years."

She's trying to give them a plausible explanation to grasp, but they aren't buying it. Sarah looks like she's about to haul back and punch Steffi. Steve's trying to stay calm, but his eyes deceive him. They're turning stormy. Rob bobs in the water, looking completely perplexed. Keiko frowns.

"No," she says. "We have to stay together. I'm sure of it. And I don't want to stay here."

"But you don't like the sea, Keiko. Now that we can control Pooky, wouldn't it be easier to stay here?" My voice sounds sticky-sweet and pleading. The cold stare she fixes on me makes me disgusted with myself for trying to coerce her this way.

"No," she says with a firm resolution I've never heard in her voice before. "We stay here, we immunize the other kids, and we get off this island. Together."

Steffi frowns. "We don't owe anything to those kids."

"Hey!" Matt says. "Those kids are my friends."

"So? They chased you here, didn't they? You don't belong with them anymore."

"No," Keiko says again. "That's not how it works, Steffi. Just because you think so doesn't mean that's how it's gonna be."

Sarah nods. "I agree with Keiko. You can't spite those kids because you think they're turning into The Others. We're stronger than they are. We can hold our ground. We need to make peace with them."

"You go ahead," Steffi says. "Make peace with them all you want. Meanwhile, Jack and I will go and do what he needs to do."

Now Steve frowns. "And why do *you* get to go, Steffi, while dooming the rest of us to stay here?"

This is getting out of control. "Listen," I say. "I don't feel good about leaving those kids to deal with Pooky. And I don't feel great at all about asking you to stay. But I need to go. And Steffi needs to come with me. I can't explain why, except I *feel* it. This is what needs to happen."

"Well," Sarah says, smacking her large fist into the water and biting off her words, "that clinches it then, doesn't it? Let's all roll over because high and mighty Jack Outrigger *feels* we should."

"No," I plead, "Sarah...that isn't what I meant..."

But Sarah's already storming out of the water and up the beach. Pooky hisses at her from the grass. She's so mad, she yells at him and kicks sand in his direction.

"Great," Steve says, lunging for the shore and the shield that Sarah has bypassed in her rage. "Jack, we aren't done with this conversation."

Rob gulps some water. "Jack...do you really think this is the best way?"

Keiko turns angrily towards him. "You aren't going for this, are you?"

"I dunno...I mean, if there's a way for Jack to find the way out and come back for us...you *would* come back for us, right, Jack?"

I don't know what the hell will happen if we leave, but I nod. "Of course."

"Well then, maybe it wouldn't be so bad..."

His voice trails off as Keiko lets out a barrage of what must be Japanese swear words and swims after Steve.

"Well, that didn't go well," Steffi murmurs.

Bhasker touches her shoulder. "I understand, if it helps. I'll stay here."

She gives him a surprised glance. "You will?"

"Yes. I can immunize the other kids while you're gone."

Frank nods. "I'd rather go with you. But it isn't my place really to tell you what to do. And if I had a choice, I'd rather head to your old island to find my brother than go with you guys. Too bad we can't build another boat."

I turn to Matt. "And you?"

He shakes his head. "I dunno. It seems weird, what's happening here. We all used to get along. And now...everyone seems to be splitting up. When we left Goliath's room the other day, after the lightning storm, the other kids *did* chase us, like Frank predicted. I didn't really think they'd go that far, but they really wanted the weapons. The split is fairly even. Six of the kids chased us, the others didn't. I never thought we'd become enemies. And now...look at your group."

"We're not enemies," I say. "We're just having a little misunderstanding."

"I don't think so," Matt says. "There's a rift in our group, now there's one in yours."

Steffi shakes her head. "This is starting to sound more and more like The Others on Mukade Island all the time."

I agree. This island is becoming divided. The schism is happening all over again. But if it's happening in our group, am I on the side of right? Or are Steffi and I becoming "The Others"?

We wade towards the shore. Pooky still rustles in the grass, and Steve has taken the shield back into the tunnel. Spike soars towards us, chirping.

"He's been busy all afternoon," I whisper, motioning to the bat. "I think he's making some of the tunnels into safe zones. Some for us, some for them."

Steffi frowns. "Like us and The Others on Mukade Island. Wouldn't it be nice if he made the whole beach into a safe zone where Pooky couldn't get in?"

"I'm not sure if he could do that."

"He needs barriers to make a safe zone, right? The beach is a natural barrier, even though it's a long one. If Spike could make it a safe zone, Pooky couldn't get to it. And then he couldn't get any of the kids. He can't throw a web the distance of the grass to the sea."

Spike chirps softly. "No," I say. "He won't do that. Pooky needs to eat too."

Steffi chokes. "That's horrible, Jack."

"Spike said it, not me." I scrutinize the little bat fluttering near my ear. "Y'know, the bats help us, but only so much. If you think about it, the bats are part of the whole plan of these islands, same as the mukade, same as the spider. I don't think Spike will help us kill Pooky at all. He doesn't want the monster dead. That isn't how it's supposed to work."

Steffi narrows her eyes. "How what's supposed to work, Jack?"

I shrug. "This place. Whoever or whatever created it, they put us all here for a reason, and they've put the mukade and bats and spider and God knows what else here for us to figure out. Maybe all this is a test."

She laughs. "A test?"

"Yeah. It's like a game, don't you see? Whoever can figure out the secrets to this place, they'll be victorious. And they'll get out of here."

"Well," Steffi says, "Let's hope that's us. I want to go home, Jack. I want out of this place."

I nod. "Me too."

I turn around and watch the waves roll up and smash down. Up and down, up and down, and suddenly wooziness overtakes me.

"You okay?" Steffi asks me. Her voice drifts through my head, but muffled, as if she were far away. The undulating waves fill my vision. I'm falling...falling into the warm sand.

I don't remember anything after that.

BLUE DOTS

When I wake, I find I'm lying in our tunnel on a pile of grass. Steffi lies next to me, asleep. Asleep or, like me, unconscious. Rob is sprawled next to her. So is Frank. Keiko sits next to me, a worried expression plastered on her face.

"Thank God," she whispers as I shake my groggy head. "I thought nobody'd ever wake up."

"What is it?" I murmur. "What's going on?"

Steve comes over. "Steffi and Rob dragged you back in here a few hours ago. They yelled for us and we shielded you from Pooky and got everyone into the tunnel. You were passed out. Then, one by one, the others fell into this weird coma. You were breathing normally, so we knew you weren't dead. But we couldn't wake you."

"I'm so sorry," I say.

"It's okay," Keiko whispers. "It's probably a side-effect from the blue dots. You know, like what happened on Mukade Island when we got bit by the mukade."

I grasp her hand. "No, I mean before..in the sea. I've been so worried about telling you..."

Keiko's other hand gently brushes my forehead. "Don't worry about that now. We've all been talking. We'll figure it out."

She holds a bowlful of seawater to my lips, and I take a grateful gulp. The water slides down my parched throat. I struggle to a sitting position and check out the others. They look peaceful enough, like they're having a nice sleep with good dreams. I don't remember dreaming anything myself, but there weren't any nightmares either.

Spike flies over to my shoulder and chirps.

Interesting.

Steve leans closer. "What did he say?"

"The pond water did it. Or, more precisely, the blue cells that live in it. They were busy working."

"Working how?"

"I'm not sure. Spike says that after we drink the stuff, we eventually go into a hibernation for a couple of hours while the blue cells work in your body. To do what, I don't know yet. But Spike doesn't think it's anything bad."

Keiko frowns. "But we're already all immune to the seawater now. Most of the island kids are too. Sarah's been taking them up there all day."

I don't know why, but that information makes me feel so much better. Even if it doesn't change their attitude, I'm glad the island kids can now benefit from the seawater.

"So, if we're already immune to the seawater," Steve says, "I wonder what the blue things are doing?"

Bhasker, who huddles against the tunnel wall, suddenly straightens up. "It's the lightning," he says.

"What?"

"The lightning. Those blue dots make you immune to the effects of lightning. You drink the water, go into a trance, and by the time you awake, the lightning won't have any effect on you."

"You didn't drink any," I say. "When we put you into that water, the blue things just swum around you, and you got better."

"True, but that was because the lightning *already* affected me. It hasn't affected you yet. The blue dots are made of lightning. You had to drink some to get the same result. Now they've made a change in you. You know what I think?"

I shake my head.

"I think we don't have to hide from the lightning any more. Any of us. It won't have any effect now."

"Yeah, two problems with that theory," Steve says. "For one, Pooky has lived right next to that pond for years, and he still has to hide in the tunnels when the lightning storm comes. And Goliath too."

"Maybe Pooky's never drunk from the pond," Steffi says.

Frank nods. "Bhasker might be right. Remember when I was telling you about Ramon? About how the lightning didn't affect him at all the second time he got caught in it?"

"We'll test it," Bhasker says. "Next lightning storm, we just won't go in."

"And if it doesn't work?" I say. "We'll end up dead. Like…"

I don't want to say her name. Bhasker takes a deep breath.

"Yes, like Malika," he finishes for me. "But I'm willing to try. We don't all have to do it. If it doesn't work for me, hopefully you can take me to the pond and I'll be cured. If it's too much, well…"

He gazes down the tunnel, to where we buried Malika. He'd like to be with her, I think.

Hopefully he wants to survive even more.

<<<>>>

The others wake up, one by one. They listen to Bhasker's theory. Everyone acknowledged that they had drunk the pond water, so that part makes sense. We're reacting to the blue microbes. They're doing something to us, changing us somehow.

But whether they'll immunize us to the lightning is up for debate. Frank looks hopeful.

"If we're immune to the lightning, once we kill Pooky, the island will be ours," he says.

108

"I don't think we should kill Pooky," I say.

Steffi sits up. "Why the holy hell not?"

"I don't know. If we get the bells on him, people can hear him coming."

"Yeah, but is that what's best for Pooky?" Steve says. "Think about it. It's like putting a rat trap out for a rat. The rat gets caught in it then slowly starves to death. If we put the bells on Pooky, and he can't catch any more kids, won't he die anyway? But die a long-suffering death? Wouldn't it be better to put the awful thing out of his misery now?"

I hadn't thought of that. "Maybe," I say. "Or maybe he has another food source he survives on when he can't catch a kid."

Frank nods. "The slugs."

"Anyway, is it worth it?" Matt asks, shuddering. He's remembering the feel of that sticky web wrapped around him, I'm sure. "Is it worth taking our chances?"

"I vote for killing the spider," Frank says.

Matt nods. "Me too. Better him than us."

I shake my head. "Something tells me we either shouldn't, or can't, kill Pooky. I don't think we should mess with him."

Sarah, who has returned from taking the last group of island kids up to the pond, gives a harsh laugh. "It isn't up to you to decide, Jack."

"I didn't say it was. I just have this feeling…"

"You have a lot of 'feelings'. Doesn't mean they're right."

She hasn't let the confrontation in the sea go. Keiko has, I think, or at least her innate desire to heal and nurture has overridden her anger while we've been comatose, but Sarah seems as mad now as earlier. She has a point, but I feel my teeth start to grind in annoyance. *Calm, Jack. Keep calm.* I try another tack, although I already know she won't like it.

"Listen, the main problem we have right now isn't Pooky. It's the kids who want the weapons and the boat so they can get off this rock."

Steffi nods. "And now you've immunized 'em, they have more of an incentive to take those things."

"No," Matt says, almost hopefully. "Now they're immunized, we're friends again. They're happy."

Sarah shifts from one leg to the other. "I dunno...they were thankful but not too thankful, if you know what I mean. Steffi...well...she may be right about that."

Now it's Matt's turn to look mutinous. "No, they're good again. If we kill Pooky, everything will go back to how it was."

"I don't think so," Steffi argues. "We can eliminate the main issue by taking the canoe and leaving, *then* they might be more willing to cooperate."

I nod. "What we really need to focus on now is getting the canoe fixed."

Sarah frowns, but not as deeply. "So you can go."

"Well...yes. And if it isn't before the next lightning strike, we can test out Bhasker's theory. Until then, we leave Pooky alone, and we concentrate on the boat. Any objections?"

Sarah looks like she wants to object, and how, but she gives in. I guess she figures nobody's getting off this island without the canoe, and while we're fixing it, maybe she can change our minds.

But as much as I wish it, my mind is made up.

<<<>>>

Of course, the canoe is still in pieces and not doing *anybody* any good, so we refocus on how to convince Goliath to help us fix it. We'll need Spike for that. Steffi and I head off with the little bat to find the monster worm. We take the shield and map with us.

We find Goliath snoozing in his nest. "How do we wake him?" Steffi whispers. "I mean, he's been pretty patient with us so far, but what if he's cranky when he wakes up? He might be mad. Maybe we should wait until he's... what's that?"

She can't see that well in the darkness, but I can. Spike has whispered in wherever Goliath's ear is located, and he's moving. "He's ready," I say. "He'll help."

Goliath slides towards a different passage, followed by Spike. "He's heading to the tunnel that comes out near where we left the canoe," I say.

"Damn, we still have the outrigger in *our* tunnel," Steffi says. "We need to get it down there before Goliath gets annoyed and leaves. You know, if we finally ever do find our way home, I'm never crawling into a tunnel again."

We bolt back up the tunnel and grab the outrigger. Frank and Sarah help us carry it down the beach. Matt follows with the shield, although it's midday and Pooky should be asleep. Steve grabs the axe and heads out with us. "You might need the axe to do a little finishing work to the canoe," he says.

"If we get the outrigger there quick," I huff as we plow through the sand, "we could have it fixed in no time. We could be out of here by tomorrow."

"That soon, huh?" Sarah grunts. She doesn't elaborate.

"Well, we don't need to gather any provisions. We've figured out how to deal with Pooky, Spike's made more safe zones for everybody, everyone can now swim in the sea, and everyone's hopefully now immune to the lightning strikes."

"We don't know that yet," Matt says. "We haven't tested that theory out."

"Yeah, I'd rather know if that's true or not before we leave here," Steffi says. "What if we're out on the sea and get caught in that storm, and we *aren't* protected? We'll be fried to a crisp."

"Or go completely mad," Matt adds.

"Uh-oh," Sarah mutters, plowing to a halt in the sand.

"What?"

"We've got company. Look ahead."

I expect to see Pooky, but what I do see is worse.

Six kids barrel up the beach towards us. Six. And we have six. An even match. But we have weapons too. And we'll use them, if it comes down to it.

Steffi has her knife. Matt has the shield. Steve has the axe. We drop the outrigger in the sand and steel ourselves. The kids stop about five feet in front of us. We peruse each other.

Now, I never got to know the island kids that well, but these are the meanest-looking in the group. Four boys and two girls. Aaron is in front, his once-worshipful look replaced with a hard determination. He flexes his one arm. The kid next to him is smaller but blockier; he looks like he's been in fights before and knows how to handle himself. The other two boys are thin as twigs and look nervous. The two girls remind me of Marissa. Large. Mean. The biggest, her name is Clara if I remember right, steps forward.

"Clara..."Matt whispers, "...what are you doing?"

She ignores him and fixes her eyes on Steffi. "Give us the knife."

"Sure thing, sister. Would you like our other weapons too?"

Steffi smirks and stands her ground, holding the knife out, ready to strike. She's attacked a girl before. She won't hesitate to do it now. She eyes Clara, trying to find her opponent's weakness. All these kids have something. Clara looks healthy enough. Frank leans forward and whispers, "Deviated septum. Sinus problems. Won't help you much in a fight."

"Think you're smart, don't you?" Clara snarls. "We want your weapons. Now. Matt, hand that thing over."

Now's the time. If Matt is going to turn traitor, we can't stop him. I remember Little Mike, from Mukade Island. How we trusted him, and he turned traitor in the end. We had never suspected him. I stare at Matt, my stomach flipping. Tears drip down his cheeks.

But he doesn't let us down. "No," he says. He sounds calm, reasonable, even with the tears. He addresses the two boys hiding behind Aaron. "Rafael, Terry, you don't have to stay with them. You can come over to our side. We're friends... right?"

"Shut up," Clara snarls, shoving one of the boys backwards as he tries to answer. "They're on our side, not yours."

Matt tries again. "But...we're all immune now. There isn't any reason to fight."

"Yes there is. There's one canoe and seventeen kids. No way we'll all fit. And we aren't getting left behind."

Steffi's eyes flick toward Sarah. "Told you it was a bad idea to immunize 'em."

Clara ignores her statement. "If you won't give us the weapons, we'll take them."

Sarah straightens up. Her eyes blaze with anger. "There's six of you and six of us, and we're the ones with the weapons. You really think you're gonna win?"

"We'll see," Clara says, and before we can react, she lunges for Steffi. A sickening crack echoes in my ears. Steffi screams and falls to the ground. Clara retreats, the knife shining in her hand.

DECISIONS

The island kids don't hang around to see what will happen next. They take off as if the devil is after them, which, if Steffi could move, would be true. But she is crumpled on the ground, holding her wrist. We group around her.

"Go after them!" she screams, tears spilling down her cheeks.

Sarah plows down the beach, but the kids are too far up the shore for her to get close. They duck down a tunnel and Sarah halts so fast she almost falls headfirst in the sand. She trudges back.

"Damn Spike. He made safe zones all right. Not sure if that was one, but I wasn't gonna risk it.

The knife is lost. Steffi still has the jeweled scabbard strapped around her waist, but the island kids weren't interested in that. They wanted the knife. And probably the axe too, but they weren't going to stick around long enough for a fight. Their plan was to ambush, grab, and go.

Steffi's wrist is broken. She is more pissed off over losing the knife than she is worried about the rapidly swelling wrist. If we weren't holding her back, she'd be off after the island kids like a shot, but we manage to talk some sense into her.

"Get her back to Keiko," I tell Steve. "Take the shield and we'll take the axe down to the canoe."

"What about Pooky?" Steve says.

"Pooky isn't going to get anywhere near Goliath. We'll be okay."

Steffi protests, but follows Steve back to our tunnel. I now wish we had used the tunnel to get to the canoe instead of the beach. We chose the beach because getting that outrigger through the tight tunnels would be trickier than out in the open, but now I'm kicking myself for choosing the more dangerous path.

Goliath and Spike wait by the canoe. We lug the broken outrigger into our safe zone and position it next to its other half. Goliath strokes his tail up and down the two pieces until they are cocooned in a hard, unbreakable (we hope) shell. We pick up the fixed outrigger. It is as light now as it was before Goliath used his glue. The stuff adds no weight at all.

With Goliath's generous help we reattach the outriggers. Instead of tying the whole contraption together with vines, Goliath solidifies the structure with a nice coat of his special shellac.

"It'll take a gang of Pookys to break *that* boat," I say, gazing upon it.

"Does this mean it's ready to go?" Sarah says, staring at the boat.

"Yup."

Sarah frowns. "Jack, the island kids haven't changed. Seems they've gotten worse. You know they're going to try for the boat, they as good as said so. You aren't gong to leave us here. Steffi's wrist is now broken, so she won't be too good in a fight, and so help me God..."

She doesn't have to finish the sentence, the threatening look is enough.

"There's no way we're all gonna fit in the canoe, Sarah," I say.

"No, there isn't. But you don't get to choose who goes and who stays. I hope I'm making myself clear."

"Listen," Frank says in his soothing voice. "Let's not discuss this now. Let's go make sure Steffi is okay. She isn't going anywhere with a broken wrist."

<<<>>>

Steffi is in a foul mood. She's in pain and she's crazy with rage at the island kids for stealing her knife. "Why the hell do they want it that badly?" she asks. "I mean, it's great to have a knife, but they've gotten along fine without one until now."

"In that case, why do you want it back so bad?" Bhasker asks.

Steffi growls at him. I think I know why. She is obsessed with the knife. She's unnaturally attached to it, to the point that it probably isn't good for her. Maybe losing the knife is a good thing. I make the mistake of pointing this out.

"That knife," Steffi says, grinding her teeth and glaring at me, "is a treasure. We *need* it. I don't know what for, but it has some purpose. Don't you feel that Jack? You're so good at guessing what we have to do. You want to go off and find this person because you know he'll help us out. You have a plan. Well, the plan includes that knife, whether you realize it or not. We found it for a reason. Just like the other things we found."

She takes a breath, trying to calm down. "Each object has a purpose. The black powder cured the mukade bites. The telescope helped us navigate the sea. The map lets us know where we're supposed to go. And when we got to this island, we found things too. The bells and shield are for controlling the spider. The map shows the tunnels and how to get around."

"And the axe?" Rob asks, holding it up.

Steffi contemplates it. "The axe is like the knife. We need it, but we're not sure what for yet. We don't need it *here*. It comes in handy for defending ourselves and stuff, but I think its purpose lies elsewhere. Not on this island. Just like the knife."

I sit down and mull over what Steffi has said. She might be right. These boxes that we keep finding, they have a dual purpose. Some items are used to conquer whichever island we're on. The other items, maybe we do need them for later.

What we need to use them *for* is the mystery.

"If Steffi's job was to guard the knife," Rob says, "then my job is to guard the axe." His fist curls around its handle. "I'm the Guardian of the Axe, Jack. I need to go with you in the boat."

I sink against the wall. "Fine, Rob."

He eyes me in surprise. "Really? I didn't think you'd go for that."

He smiles, like he made a funny joke, but I can't laugh. Maybe it has something to do with losing the knife, maybe more to do with Sarah's threat, but suddenly leaving with Steffi doesn't seem that important. And Rob, for some insane reason, is making complete sense. Or maybe I'm just tired.

"What, so now you're switching tactics?" Sarah says, looking as surprised as Rob.

"Maybe. But I think Steffi's right. We've gotta get that knife back. We can't leave this island without it."

<<<>>>

With much screaming and cursing from Steffi, Keiko manages to set the bones in her wrist. She wraps the wrist in grass. We take Steffi down to Goliath's chamber, and he kindly spreads some goo over the grass. It hardens into a nice cast.

"How long does she have to wear it?" Rob asks.

Keiko shrugs. "I don't know. I hope I put the bones right."

"I hope so too," Steffi says. "Thanks Keiko. I know I cussed at you when you were setting it. I didn't mean any of the bad things I said."

Keiko grins. "I know you didn't. You're welcome."

"I broke my wrist once, when I was a kid," Frank says. "I think I kept the cast on for six weeks or so."

"How're we going to get it off once the bones heal?" Steffi says, contemplating the cast. "This stuff is pretty hard."

"In the emergency room, they used a little saw on my cast," Frank says. "But we don't have one of those here."

"We've got the axe," Rob says. "I bet that'll work."

Steffi shudders. "Sure, unless it takes my whole arm off with it."

<<<>>>

In the morning, Steve, Keiko, Matt, and Sarah lie comatose on the floor. Bhasker, although he went into the pond the same time as they did, seems fine. He claims it's because he was already comatose for so long already.

We leave them there and head for the sea. We're almost finished with our morning swim when we spot two island kids running down the beach. They motion wildly to us. I recognize them as the two boys hiding behind Aaron yesterday, and head to shore.

"We've escaped," one of them gasps. "Save us!"

I glance up the empty beach. "Do they know you've gone?"

"No, but they will soon. They're still asleep. Please, can we come into your tunnel? We know they can't follow us in there."

"You can try," I say. If these kids are sincere, they can access our safe zone. If they aren't, the safe zone will repel them.

They make it into the tunnel and huddle in the back corner. "You're on our side now," Rob says, grinning at the scared boys. "You're safe."

They tell us their story. It sounds so eerily like how The Others functioned, I wonder if the kids got the idea from the stories we told them. Or maybe, that's how it works. Once an island is divided, one group stays reasonably sane, and the other group gets all barbaric.

The two kids, Rafael and Terry, have become no better than slaves. They're picked on. They're forced to sleep in the less comfortable areas. They aren't allowed to use the toilet.

"How can people be so cruel, and for no reason?" Bhasker asks.

118

I shrug. "Maybe it has something to do with the game."

Bhasker frowns. "The what?"

I try to explain. "Bhasker, I haven't wondered much why we were sent to this place. I've been more focused on how to escape it. But...well...what if we aren't being punished? I mean, we are, but what if the only reason they put us all here is because this is all some sort of weird game? And whoever can get to the end of it, wins?"

"Yeah, but wins what?" Frank says. "That's what I want to know."

"So..." Rob says, squinting, which usually means he's trying hard to follow the conversation, "...you think maybe we're like rats in a maze? Like somebody's deliberately put all these puzzles in place in the hopes that we'll eventually figure it out?"

"Yeah," I say. "Something like that."

"And maybe," Frank adds, "putting some kind of schism in place is part of it. The kids on your island were already separated. But maybe it's just starting here."

"But why?" Rob says.

Frank frowns. "I don't know, but maybe..." and here he pauses, and I wonder if he's thinking about his brother, Mike, "...maybe they're sorting out the ones they *want* to win. Maybe this is the point where the divide begins between who goes on and who stays behind."

Rob turns to me. "But we're the good ones, and Jack wants to leave *us* behind."

I shake my head. "I don't want to. I just felt like I had to."

He sighs. "I guess I still don't get it. Why would somebody go to all this trouble?"

"I don't know, Rob, I'm simply guessing. Who knows?"

The others start to wake up. While they're getting their bearings, Steffi asks Rafael and Terry about the knife.

"Why did they want it so bad?" she says.

Terry shrugs. "Clara wanted it. I don't know why. She's twice as scary now she has it. She keeps threatening to use it on us if we don't do exactly what she says."

"She wants it to keep the others in line," Frank says.

"Maybe she'll try and fight Pooky with it," Rafael says, his eyes twinkling. "She's full enough of herself, she might think she can do it. I don't think she'd win, do you?"

Steffi shakes her head. "I don't want Pooky getting that knife either."

"They want the axe and the shield, too," Rafael says.

"Of course they do," I say. "Frankly, they can have the shield when we leave. But not before."

I wish I hadn't said anything. Their haunted eyes perk up with hope. "Now that we're immune to the seawater, we can all get across the sea, can't we?" Rafael says.

Steffi's eyes rest on me. My stomach lurches. Now we have eleven kids who want off. Even if we all do want to go, the canoe will never hold that many.

GOLIATH

Steffi and I seem to have our best talks in the sea. There's something about the seawater that calms you down, makes you more reasonable, less prone to anger. Even the confrontation we had yesterday, when we all argued about everyone staying and Steffi and I going alone, could have been much more confrontational if it hadn't happened in the sea.

Now Steffi swims up to me. The others are silently floating farther off, maybe contemplating everything that's happened in the last couple of days. She glances at them, then says, "What made you change your mind?"

"About what?" I say.

"About taking everyone else. You've gone from insisting they don't come to trying to figure out how to get everyone off...I can tell that's what you're thinking now."

"And what do *you* think?"

"I dunno. I did think you were right...about us going alone. But something's changed here. It's like, since we had an actual fight with those kids..." here she contemplates her broken wrist, "...the sides have been drawn, hard and sharp. And now that they're drawn, even if we get rid of Pooky this place is no longer a safe haven. Our side can't stay here, any more than they could have stayed on Mukade Island."

121

I nod. "That's what I think is happening. It's all some weird game. Like we've been put here on purpose and our conditions are manipulated, to try and steer us in some direction. I'm still positive that at some point we have to go on alone and leave everyone else behind. That feeling is so insistent. But this place isn't it. It isn't the ultimate safe zone. Look what it's done...it's almost divided us, too."

Steffi nods. "We need to stick together. At least until we find an island where there is no evil insect and no rotten kids."

"Well, the canoe is as ready as we're going to get it, but there's one problem. There's no way we can fit everyone in it. Not without the rafts."

We call the others over to discuss it. "We could try and get some wood from Pooky's nest," Frank says, motioning to himself, Matt, Rafael, and Terry. "There isn't enough room in that canoe for us, but if we can scrape together at least one raft, we'll be able to come too."

"What about the other kids?" Matt says. "They betrayed us, but we can't leave with everything and not give them a chance against Pooky."

"Well," Steffi says, "we *could* leave them the shield. I'm pretty sure its only function is to control Pooky. It won't do us much good to lug it across the sea. We sure don't have much space for it. And we can leave the map because it shows the kids all the tunnels. But we need to get the knife back from 'em first."

Frank nods. "That sounds fair."

They head to the pond to try their luck with Pooky. Spike flies with them, to act as a warning signal. I'm doubtful there will be enough salvageable wood left to fix a raft, but it's worth a shot. Nobody can figure out any other solution.

The rest of us take the last of our provisions to the canoe using our safe-zone tunnels.

"I'll be so glad to leave this island," Steffi says as we walk. "As soon as we get the knife back, we're outta here."

"What about your wrist?" I ask.

"What about it? It can heal just as fast on the sea as it can here. Goliath's cast is so strong I can even use it already. And I think the seawater is helping it to heal. I bet it heals pretty damn quick."

We exit the tunnel. It opens on to the beach to the right of the canoe. Even if Pooky is out, he'll be hard put catching us in this small distance. Our circle is over one small dune.

We climb to the dune, Pooky nowhere in sight. Steffi looks down into our circle. She screams.

I stare at the empty space where the canoe once lay.

It's gone.

"Holy hell," Steve whispers.

"How?" Sarah asks, looking dumbfounded.

I shake my head. Steffi is so angry she can't answer, so I take a deep breath.

"They took it. Must've been a few minutes before we got here, Steve. I was down here not two hours ago, lining the canoe with grass so it won't be so hard on our backs."

"Look," Steffi says, pointing. Way out to sea, bobbing past the breakers, is our canoe, although it's too far to make out who's on it. And I can't use the telescope because...damn it...I'd already packed it in the canoe.

"It's too far away to swim out and catch it," Bhasker says.

"But how?" Steve asks. "They couldn't get into our safe zone. Could they?"

"They learned it from Pooky," I say. "*They* couldn't enter that circle, but they knew they could throw something in and drag the boat out."

"Impossible," Steve says.

"No," Sarah says, "not impossible. Think about it. Pooky could throw his web into our safe zones. Why couldn't those kids throw a net?"

"Where would they find a net?" Keiko asks.

"Are you kidding? This island is made of nothing but long, wavy grass. They just had to tie that stuff together."

I nod. "I think they might have made a rope long enough so they could walk around the outer edge of the circle and surround the canoe. Then all they had to do was pull from either side and move it through the sand. It's a pretty light boat. If they made the rope strong enough, they could've dragged it. And once a part of the canoe was sticking out of the circle, all they had to do was grab it and pull it out."

I sit down, exhausted. And depressed. The canoe is gone. Our one way off the island, and the other kids took it.

"We've gotta follow that boat," Steffi says, looking murderous.

I have to laugh. "How? Swim? Float on our backs?"

"Jack, they've got the knife. You can bet they took it with them."

Steve shades his eyes with one hand. "I can barely make it out, but I don't think they're all on it. I think they've left some kids behind. Maybe the knife is still here."

"No, it isn't. You know as well as I do they took it. They stole the knife then stole the canoe. Damn it, we were stupid. We didn't even guard it. We thought that little safe zone would be enough."

"We should've made it bigger," I agree. "We should've gone back to the safe zone and widened the circle over the last few days, but we didn't Steffi, and the boat is gone. We need to think of what we're going to do now."

"Build another one," Steffi says.

"With what? Grass?" Rob says, laughing. "What're we gonna do, weave it together and hope it floats?"

I suck in my breath. The kids fall quiet. All I can hear are the waves rolling up the beach. Steffi and I stare at each other. My eyes are probably as wide as hers. We're both thinking the same thing.

"It'll work," Steffi says, breaking the silence.

"A grass boat? You're serious?" Rob says.

"It *will* work," I say. "All we need is Goliath's glue."

"Just like the sand bowls," Steffi says. "Goliath's slime trail in the sand made 'em. They're solid, they don't disintegrate in the sea. They're light as anything. All we have to do is gather a bunch of grass together, convince Goliath to shellac it, and we have a perfect floating raft. It shouldn't take long at all."

"And we can all leave on it," Terry says, eyes shining.

"I suppose...if we made it big enough..." Steve says.

Rob frowns. "Why couldn't we? If the island is really splitting us into factions, then the bad faction just stole our canoe and skedaddled. If any other kids are left, they must've been like Rafael and Terry, or like Bhasker and Malika...forced to be on that side. And if that's the case, they should leave with us. Every single one. If Goliath can do what you say, there's no reason we can't make a *flotilla* of rafts if we want to."

"That'll take forever," Steffi says, "and the bad kids have half the treasures. Damn it, they have *all* the treasures now except the shield and axe. Even our map was on that boat."

We break our discussion as Pooky's screams reverberate across the island. I can't tell if they're screams of anger or victory. I sure hope Frank's bunch is okay.

<<<>>>

The grass raft idea solidifies when we spot two island kids struggling up the beach, peering anxiously into the grass, nervous about the now quiet spider. I recognize the girl with the limp, Nadia, who we rescued on our first day. A small boy trails her. He must be at least fifteen to be here, but he looks all of ten. He stares around with quiet eyes, and I realize he must have Down's Syndrome. He smiles at us.

"I'm Zane."

"Hi, Zane, Keiko says.

Zane frowns. "Where is Frank?"

"Up at the pond," I say.

"Pooky?"

"Up there too, I guess."

"Pooky sometimes screams when he's about to start a hunt," Nadia says. "We got worried."

"They should be back soon," Keiko says. "Come on in the tunnel. You'll be safe there."

We take them in. Their story is similar to Terry's and Rafael's. They hadn't been able to escape as easily.

"They told us to wait in the tunnel," Nadia says, "and threatened to hurt us if we dared to leave it. But then they were gone for so long, we thought maybe..."

"They're long gone," Steffi says. "They took our canoe."

Nadia's face brightens. "Oh. Good. Then they won't be back."

"Yeah, well, good for them, bad for us."

"But," Keiko says, smiling gently, "we think we've found a way to get us all off the island. We're just waiting for Frank and the others."

"They've been gone an awfully long time," Steve murmurs. "I hope Pooky isn't quiet because..."

He doesn't finish the sentence, but now it's stuck in all our brains. If somehow Pooky overcame the kids, he'd be busy right now bundling them up and stuffing them in that bone-ridden lair of his. And the shield...how would we ever get the shield back?

The shield. Before I even mourned the possible death of three friends, I had worried about the shield. The idea that I could be so cold forces my stomach into a nervous clench. I take a deep breath.

"They're okay," I say. "We'd have heard from Spike if they weren't. We just have to wait."

We wait. And wait. Nobody wants to start collecting grass, not with the silent spider possibly creeping about. All we can do is sit in the tunnel, growing more anxious.

126

Steffi's so nervous she begins pacing up and down the length of the tunnel.

"The lights are gonna turn off soon," she murmurs.

"Wait," Steve says. "I hear something."

Footsteps. In a mass, we surge to the tunnel entrance where a tired-looking Frank is leading Matt, Terry, and Rafael, all stumbling around like drunks.

"What the hell happened?" Steffi shouts.

"They all went into comas, about the same time," Frank says. "I had to let them lie there in the grass until they came to. Man, I don't want to go through something like that again. It happened right in the middle of one of those trails, and then the spider got all silent and stealthy, and I couldn't figure out which way to face. If it weren't for Spike's chirps every time he spotted Pooky's legs, we'd have been done for, I think."

"Well, it's a damn good thing you got here before the lights went off," Steffi says, sighing.

"I didn't get any poles," he says. "I had enough trouble trying to herd these three back without throwing poles into it."

"That's okay," I say. "We have a better plan."

Everyone's too exhausted and frazzled to start working on the rafts so close to light's-out, so we wait to collect grass until morning. Spike stands as lookout for Pooky. Rob walks around us, shield in hand. Everyone else pulls as many of the long purple blades as our arms will hold, piling them on the sand.

"What do we do with the grass?" Steffi asks. "Are we going to lay it out and have Goliath glue the whole pile?"

Steve, who knows the most about boats, says, "That would be the fastest. But not the strongest. I think we should bundle the grass into sheaves, so they kind of resemble logs. Then we can give the boats some sides instead of having flat rafts. We can also put some sheaves under the rafts to buoy them up. Kind of like a catamaran."

"Why do we need sides?" Frank asks.

"Well, we ran into a sea monster once," Steve says. "We were on the rafts and one good wave from its tail was enough to send Bhasker right over the edge. If we have sides on this raft, we'll have a little more protection."

"I agree," Steffi says, shuddering.

We bundle the grass into sheaves and tie the sheaves together with more grass. Getting the grass together takes most of the day, but by evening, when we hear Pooky's "I'm hungry" scream echoing across the island, we have enough sheaves to make three large rafts, which Steve says will hold everyone.

"Why don't we just make one big one?" Rob says.

"Too hard to steer, and I'm not sure about the floatability," Steve says. "I'm comfortable with the sizes we have. We can get four to five kids easily on each raft, with enough room to store some fruit, even."

"Now we need Goliath," Steffi says, "to finish 'em up before morning. We should get off this island as fast as possible. They've got way too much of a head start."

I shake my head. "We don't even know which way they're going, Steffi," I say.

"They're going with the current. We will too. We gotta catch them before the current takes them too far."

"What'll happen then?" Rob says. "They've got our stuff."

Sarah, who's lugged more grass than anyone today, wipes her brow. "There'll be a fight, for sure. They aren't gonna give back our treasures willingly."

Rob frowns. "How the hell do we fight kids on the open sea?"

Sarah's face hardens. "It's like King of the Hill. Whoever pushes the most kids of the opposite side into the sea wins."

"The sea won't hurt 'em none," Rob says.

"Not unless we leave them there and they drown in it."

She says this in a calm, even, rational voice. That type of voice used to give me the chills. I could never understand how easy these kids could dismiss somebody once they're gone. Like they never really existed in the first place. Sarah's bland tone as she discusses the imminent demise of a bunch of kids who really didn't ask for this in the first place, should start those chills right up again, but they refuse to come. I guess I understand it now. If it comes to those kids or us, we have to prevail. Even if it means the kids in that boat are doomed to die.

Those are the rules of the game. I just wish I could still feel a little trepidation about it.

"What do we do now?" Keiko whispers. "We need to get Goliath down here."

I nod. "Steffi and I will go look for Goliath. The rest of you, go take a dip. Get something to eat."

We trudge through the tunnels, Spike fluttering above my head, his claws grasping my hair. We leave the other kids the shield for protection. We find a snoozing Goliath in has main chamber. He seems to be using the empty treasure box as a pillow.

"Man, I hope he doesn't mind being disturbed," Steffi whispers. "We really need to get moving."

Spike flutters over and coos. Goliath grunts, then yawns and slowly oozes towards us. "He'll help," I say.

"Great!" Steffi says, breathing a sigh of relief. It isn't until she does it that I realize how relieved I am, too. If Goliath hadn't offered to help, we'd never catch up with the canoe. We'd be stuck here forever.

"But of course, he'd help," Steffi whispers as we follow Goliath out the tunnel. "If this is all some sort of game, like you think, he'd *have* to help us, wouldn't he?"

"I suppose so," I say. "Although it's probably the last step in this island's puzzle."

"No," Steffi says. "Pooky is the last piece."

"If we're all gone," I say, "Pooky won't matter."

Steffi squeezes my shoulder. "Jack, just because we're leaving doesn't mean that new kids aren't still going to keep popping up. What happens when that first new kid gets here, and there's nobody around to help him? To let him know about Pooky? He'll be spider food for sure."

I hadn't thought about that. We'd left kids on Mukade Island. Maybe we need to do that on this island. The Others, even though they were all jerks, would at least teach any new kids about the island's secrets. Or would they? We took the powder with us when we left. It does us no good now, but it could've had some use if we'd had left it on Mukade Island.

"We should've left the powder," I mumble.

I can feel Steffi shrug. "How do we know that box we found won't regenerate itself for the next batch of kids? Somebody obviously planted it there. Means somebody could plant more powder there again, if they wanted."

I sigh. "Why does this all have to be so confusing? What is the point of any of this?"

"I know," Steffi says. "It makes no sense. But all we can do is play it out as best we can. You think anybody would volunteer to stay here, to help out the new kids?"

"Not with that monster running around," I say.

"What if we did what Keiko suggested? What if we get the bells on him?"

"That might help," I say. "But how do we do that?"

Goliath has some trouble solidifying the rafts. In the end, they aren't pretty. The goop is uneven and the rafts are a bit asymmetrical, but we take one down to the sea and it passes the float test. The sheaves of grass positioned underneath the raft buoy it up so we ride a little above the water. With the sides over a foot tall, it'll take some good wave action to flood it.

"It's stable too," Steve says. "And roomier than the outrigger canoe. We'll have a hard time flipping it."

"God, I wish we had a sail," Steffi says. "Those kids must be miles away by now."

"Floating adrift though," I say. "They have no idea where they're going."

"They've got the telescope," Steffi reminds me.

"Yeah, but ten to one none of 'em can use it. You guys couldn't."

"How do we know which direction they went?" Sarah asks.

"They went with the current. So will we. We don't have any choice without a good way to steer this thing. We'll be floating adrift out there, which I don't like much, but we have no choice."

"We need some oars before we go," Frank says. "Let's collect some more grass, real quick. We can make something to kind of steer this thing with. Then we'll be off."

Steffi looks frazzled but she agrees. Some of us run to collect handfuls of grass while Steve and Frank finish stocking the rafts with fruit.

"You really think we can trust these rafts?" Rob says as he yanks grass out by its roots. "You remember that sea monster. I bet he makes mincemeat of that thing."

Steffi laughs. "Those rafts are just as strong as the canoe, guaranteed."

Rob scoffs. "It can't be. We made these things in like a day. The old canoe took us weeks and weeks."

"Doesn't mean these aren't as strong," Steffi says.

"They're weaker, trust me. We rushed it. Maybe we should stay longer and make sure the rafts work. Maybe row one around the island a few times to make sure it won't disintegrate."

"No way," Steffi says. "Those kids are far enough ahead of us as it is. We're leaving as soon as we finish making the oars."

We keep pulling. The thick grass loosens easily from the crumbly sand, and soon we have a few armfuls. We turn around to head back to the boat, and...

"Oh no," Steffi says, dropping her load.

FIGHTING ANANSI

A huge black shadow lunges out of the grass.

Pooky.

He leaps and grabs. Keiko lets out a horrific scream before she disappears among ten hairy spider legs. As quick as he appeared, Pooky scuttles off, dragging his prey with him.

"Shield!" Rob yells. "Who has the shield?"

The shield lies in the sand, yards away from any of us. Pooky must have watched us from the tall grass, then snuck down upon us and grabbed his chance.

Rob sprints through the sand and grabs the shield. "Come on!" he yells, barreling after the lumbering spider.

I don't look back to see if anyone is following me. I chase after Rob and the spider, hoping Rob keeps his head and doesn't do anything stupid. The spider sticks to the trails—t's faster than plowing through the grass—and we follow, me panting to keep up and Rob screaming at the top of his lungs.

"Let her go, you monster!"

Pooky is fast, but he's dragging Keiko, which slows him down a bit. I'm so frightened and furious that the adrenalin kicking through me gives me feet with wings. I'm inching closer to Rob, but he is almost on top of the spider. In desperation, Pooky flings out a web. It shatters as it hits the shield.

We reach the pond. My breath exits my lungs in short, burning gasps. Rob is so close to the spider he can touch its back legs.

One of those legs flings out and smashes into the shield. The force throws Rob backwards and into the pond. The shield flies out of his hand and I lunge for it, catching it before it can sail off into the blue water. Pooky falls. He is stunned, but he hasn't turned hard, like his web did when it hit the shield. He isn't dead yet.

Rob scrambles for the shore. Steffi barrels out of the grass behind me. A funny, tinkling sound follows her.

"The bells!" she gasps. "I've got the bells."

Pooky lies, still stunned, by the pond. Keiko is moaning. I grab the shield and run around the spider. "You okay?"

She crawls between Pooky's legs, sobbing. "Did he bite you?" Rob asks, hugging her.

"Just a little. My leg is numb." Keiko tries to stand but crumples in a heap, tears running down her cheeks.

"Move her to the side," I say, as Pooky begins to twitch. "He's waking up."

"Why don't you finish him off then?" Steffi says. "You've got the shield."

"It won't kill him," I say. "It only stuns him. I think it might cause him some pain. But it isn't going to kill him, Steffi. I suppose the knife or axe would."

"Damn it, I left the axe on the beach," Rob growls. "I should've grabbed it. Knock him out again at least, would you?"

I touch one of Pooky's legs with the shield and he freezes. I glance at Keiko. She's still crying, but she's calming down. She gives the spider a hateful glare. I don't see any fear in it. I've never seen Keiko this mad, but boy is she furious now. Even more so than the day she confronted us in the sea.

"Let's get those damn bells on," she says.

Steffi stares at the bells dangling from her palm. "How do we attach 'em? There must be a way."

Spike flies to my shoulder and chirps.

"What'd he say?" Keiko says.

"He says Goliath's coming. String the bells around one of Pooky's back legs. That'll be harder for him to reach. You can snag the string on those hairy spikes."

"Oh God, you'll have to help me," Steffi says, moving towards Pooky's rear and grimacing. "I've only got one hand, plus I don't want to get near those legs."

"I'll do it," Keiko says.

She wipes her eyes, stands on shaky legs, and takes a steadying breath.

"You sure?" Steffi says. "Jack can help me."

"No, let Jack keep an eye on Pooky. I've already been wrapped in those legs once; I can stand getting close to them again."

Steffi helps her untangle the bells. Pooky twitches again and she jumps back. Keiko, out of spite or frustration, kicks the spider with her numbed leg. So does Rob. I tap Pooky again with the shield.

"Here comes Goliath," I say. "Let's see what he'll do."

"I hope something goopy," Steffi says, "because these bells won't last very long on Pooky without some glue. He'll have 'em off in no time."

Goliath lumbers over to the comatose spider. "Why don't we just kill him?" Rob says, staring at Pooky's bloated black underbelly. "I could go get the axe."

I shake my head. "I don't think we should."

"Why ever *not*?"

"I don't know. Something doesn't feel right here. Spike doesn't want us to kill him; he's told me so although I can't say why. Goliath doesn't either."

If anybody could whack Pooky right now, it'd be Goliath. But he is carefully placing drops of slime on each of Pooky's spiky hairs. The chain is on tight.

"What if Pooky tries to rip it off?" Steffi says. "That chain looks pretty flimsy."

"It's not," I say. "Whatever metal it's made of, you can be sure it's tough as nails. But I don't think Pooky will mind the bells, once they're on. I don't think he's smart enough to realize they warn others of his coming. He might even like the sound, who knows?"

Goliath plops the last bit of goo on the chain. I smack Pooky with the shield one more time for good luck, and we head back to the rafts.

"I'm sorry," Keiko says as she hobbles beside Rob.

"You couldn't help it if Pooky grabbed you," I say.

She wipes the tears off her cheeks. "I guess not. I can't wait to get out of here, Rob."

She turns to him, and he puts an arm around her shoulder. We begin the march back to the beach. Spike flies ahead. He doesn't need to keep a watch for Pooky anymore...the bells will let us know when the spider is near.

"Well," Steffi says. "Now, if new kids show up, they'll be able to hear him coming."

We reach the shore, and my stomach drops like I'm on a hundred-foot rollercoaster. The beach is completely deserted. No kids. No rafts. No nothing.

I sink to the ground, wondering what has happened now.

THE STORM

W hat the hell?" Steffi says. "Where'd everybody go?"
She tromps up the beach, scanning the horizon.
"There's the rafts. I can see them out there. Damn it, they left
without us!"

"No, they didn't," Bhasker says, ducking out of the tunnel
and walking over. "Steve and the other kids took the rafts out
to test the oars. I stayed here to let you know. We thought
about following you to fight Pooky, but then we saw Goliath
heading up that way and figured you'd be OK. So Steve decided Rob was right and we should test all the rafts while we
were waiting for you guys to return. They're rowing back now,
see?"

Steffi collapses to the ground. "I can't take much more
of this."

"We got the bells on the spider," I tell Bhasker. "I guess
we're ready to go."

"Yeah, let's go," Steffi says.

"But it'll be dark soon," Bhasker says. "In an hour, at most."

"So? They've gotten too much of a head-start on us already."

Steve glides a raft back to shore. "It works well!" he shouts.
"No leaks. Floats nice. We didn't get any water splashing into
any of the rafts, even where the waves were breaking."

"Goliath did a good job," Rob says.

"Where is he anyway?" I say. "I'd like to say goodbye."

Goliath doesn't make an appearance. I wish I had thanked him when we were tackling Pooky.

"I am still worried about new kids showing up though," Steffi admits. "We should leave the shield and some instructions. Frank, where do kids usually pop up, when they come here?"

"Right near our cave," Frank says. "In the orchard."

"Let's leave the shield and map in the cave entrance," I say. "It's the least we can do, if any other kids show up here."

"I'll do it," Matt says. Rob hands him the shield, Keiko gets the map, and Matt lopes down the beach.

"I guess that's it," I say. "Everything is done. Everyone is leaving."

"Not everyone," Bhasker whispers, glancing towards our tunnel. "I'll be right back. I want to say goodbye."

Some weird sensation ripples through my guts as I watch Bhasker trudge towards the tunnel, and I suddenly feel like I might start crying. I'd been so sure that every kid here was so immune to the feelings of loss. But I'd been mistaken. Bhasker was *still* feeling loss. He hadn't forgotten about Malika at all.

We follow him in and stare around the tunnel for the last time. Bhasker kneels near Malika's grave, kisses his fingers, and places his palm against the dirt. Then he turns to us, eyes glistening, and walks silently back to the beach. We follow. Steffi grips my hand as we step back into the light.

"Well," she says, staring at the rafts and the expectant kids, "let's get to it then."

Matt reappears, and we climb into the rafts and push away from the shore. The island fades quickly behind us. I glance back and watch Goliath lumber up the beach. His blubbery body rises into the air. It almost looks like he's searching for us so he can say goodbye.

Then he disappears. And I turn around and stare at the orange water ahead of us.

We're out to sea.

<<<>>>

So now there's thirteen of us. Steffi, Matt, Bhasker, and I share one raft. Sarah, Frank, Steve, and Terry steer another. Rob, Keiko, Rafael, Zane, and Nadia occupy the last raft.

The land disappears at an amazing pace behind us. The current here is strong. We lie back in the rafts, not bothering to paddle, waiting for darkness to arrive. Spike flutters to my lap. He stretches out his leathery wings then folds them in. I don't know what he's thinking, but if ever a bat could show signs of relief on his little face, Spike is showing it now.

"He's glad," I murmur.

"What?" Steffi asks.

"He's glad we're off Anansi Island."

Steffi grins. "Is that what we're calling it now?"

"I'm not sure what else we *can* call it," I say.

"Anansi." Steffi sighs. "Poor Malika. I still can't believe she's gone."

"Neither can I," Bhasker says.

Steffi reaches over and pats his hand. "I wish we had the telescope," she says. "It could be days before we catch up with 'em."

I squint, trying to see into the distance, like I'm hoping my eyes will suddenly have some magical power to see far away.

"I see something," Frank calls, sounding excited. "Over there."

"I see it too," Zane says.

"No...don't you get it?" Frank says. "I actually *see* something! Steffi was right. My eyesight is improving."

I'm happy for him, but when I focus my eyes on what he's pointing at, any happiness dies. I suck in my breath.

"What?" Steffi asks, straining to see.

"It's a lightning cloud!" Matt yells. "We need to get back to the island!"

Nadia whimpers. "Oh my god, we're gonna die."

There are only two oars in each boat. Steffi grabs one and I scramble for the other. We start paddling as hard as we can, trying to move the raft back the way we came.

"It's no use," Steffi said, after ten minutes of frantic paddling, where the island moves further and further from our view. "We can't fight this current."

Keiko sucks in her breath. "Here it comes," she says.

The cloud barrels towards us, long and black. Nadia begins to sob. Zane hugs her tight. Steffi stares at the ominous sky. "Maybe it'll work," she whispers.

"What?" I say.

"The water, remember? The pond water. Somebody thought it might protect us from the lightning storms. Who was it who thought that?"

I can't remember. My mind has gone blank. We watch the cloud creep closer, knowing there's no way to avoid it. Nadia whimpers and crawls under the pile of grass we had thrown into each raft last minute to use as bedding. Zane takes one last look at the black thunder clouds and follows her. So does Rob. The rest of us sit tight, watching the storm approach.

It seems like an eternity, but at the same time, time flies by. The wind hits us, soft and warm at first, then more insistent. We're close enough now to see light flashing through the clouds. Bright blue bolts smash into the sea.

"If one of those hits this boat, we're screwed," Steffi says.

"We're screwed anyway," Matt whispers. "We can't outlive this. Remember Malika."

"Yeah, but Bhasker survived," I say. "And he got better when we put him in the pond. We've got to assume whatever we drank in that pond will protect us. Spike, I sure hope you drank some of that water too."

Spike chirps. He did.

As the waves begin to swell and the dark shadows engulf our little flotilla, we all involuntarily curl up in fetal positions and huddle in the grass as best we can. Our raft rocks gently at first, but soon it flips up and down with the waves. The lightning's roar is so deafening, covering our ears does little to no good. The air vibrates with electric pulses.

But we can still think. We aren't groggy. We aren't losing our wits.

"It works," Steffi gasps. "The pond water *works*. We should be out cold by now."

Little electric prickles course through me, but Steffi's right. Instead of causing me to lose focus, the prickles feel like a gentle massage. If I weren't so scared the lightning might rip our boats to shreds, I'd even enjoy it.

A deafening crash propels the boat skyward. It falls intact, but lands hard on the surface. We grip where we can. Goliath's hardened slime is too slick to grab, the best we can do is wedge ourselves in the corners, grip a side and pray we don't get washed over. Spray soaks the raft, drenching me to the bone.

"Too close!" Steffi yells. Her hair is frizzing, and mine must look the same, but we are still thinking clearly, and that's the main thing. As long as we don't take a direct hit, we'll get through this.

The storm is moving fast. We aren't its target; it is heading for Anansi Island with a purpose and moves as quick as it can over the sea. Once it gets to the island, it will stall for a while before moving off shore again. I can already see daylight in front of us. If we can make it another few minutes...

Steffi grabs my hand and squeezes. Her eyes are shut tight and her broken arm tightens around a shivering Matt. We huddle together, counting down minutes that feel like hours. Then, suddenly, the waves cease and the rain stops. We sit up and look around.

Light dances on the rippling water. Behind us, waves rise and crash, illuminated by lightning.

"Thank God, we made it," Steffi whispers.

"Not all of us," Frank says.

I stare at where he's pointing. The new kids—Zane and Nadia—lie beneath the grass, not moving.

Steffi crawls over and lowers her ear to Nadia's chest. "She's breathing."

"She's probably passed out," Frank says. "Like we all did, after we drank the blue things."

"Yeah, but that's when the blue things are changing your body to make you immune to the lightning," Steve says, looking worried. "What if they haven't worked their magic yet? If these kids aren't immune, they'll come out like Bhasker."

"I hope not," Bhasker whispers. "Those nightmares were really horrible."

"Well," I say, sinking against the raft's sides, "it's too late to worry about that now. We'll have to see what happens when they wake up."

The lights click off. We wait out the night in silence.

<<<>>>

We're dipping up handfuls of seawater for breakfast when Frank suddenly stares out to sea, shielding his eyes. "Hey, any of you see that?"

I stare to where he's pointing. There it is. A speck in the distance, but it's definitely a boat, floating on the orange sea.

Just a boat. Empty. Either that, or the kids are piled on the bottom.

"They didn't make it," I say. "They must've took a direct hit."

"Or they're still asleep," Steffi says.

"Or comatose," Nadia says groggily from the other raft.

"Either way, it makes our job easier now, doesn't it?" I say to Steffi.

Steffi glares at me. "Did I say anything about that? What am I, a monster?"

"I'm sorry. I didn't mean anything like that," I say.

I sit back, my stomach heaving. I can't look at Steffi. Because I *hadn't* been sarcastic. I wasn't trying to egg her on. The one thought that went through my mind when I saw the canoe was...*Now it'll be easier to get the knife back.*

This time, I am the cold one. I hadn't mourned for those kids one second. I was *hoping* they had taken a direct lighting hit. The realization shakes me to the bone. My insides heave. I grab the canoe's sides and lean over, just in case. But nothing comes. The stomach settles. I slide to the floor, wiping my brow.

Sarah leans over the edge of her raft. "Are you all right, Jack?"

"I'm fine." I can't look at her. "Fine."

Even with an attempt at rowing, we don't reach the canoe until the afternoon. The kids in the bottom of it aren't comatose or sleeping. Every one is charred almost beyond recognition. This time, I do heave over the side, along with most of the other kids. Only Steffi, Sarah, and Keiko remain strong.

"What do we do with the bodies?" Steffi asks, staring into the canoe.

I can't look. "Get the treasures," I say, knowing that when it comes down to it, Steffi has a lot less queasiness when it comes to prodding dead bodies.

"We can give them a sea burial," Frank says.

"Or we can leave them in the boat," Sarah says.

"No," I say, steeling myself. "Let's be practical about this. They're dead now, they can't use it."

"We don't need it. We've got three rafts already, and they work perfectly well," Sarah says.

"It'd be a waste to let it drift away," I insist. "It'll give us space to spread out. And when the time comes, we might need it for even more kids."

"So, we have to haul it along with us?" Sarah says. "That'll be a pain."

I turn to at Steffi, wondering if she's thinking the same thing I am. That's our boat. The one we started in. The one she and I will continue in, over the sea.

She meets my gaze and gives me a little smile. "Jack and I will take the canoe."

The other kids all glance at each other. Steve finally nods. "Sounds good, Steffi."

Keiko stares into the canoe, silent tears trickling down her cheeks. "Those poor kids."

"That could've been us," Steffi says. "Thank God none of our rafts sustained a hit like that. We wouldn't have fared any better."

But the canoe did. It's burned black inside, but it doesn't have a crack in it. The outriggers are still fine. Goliath's coating is darn hard stuff.

I try not to stare at the unrecognizable corpses. The smell is bad enough, like burning hair. Steffi says a prayer for the poor kids, and she, Sarah, and Steve heave them over the side. Steffi slides the knife back in her scabbard as Steve rolls the last kid over the outrigger and into the sea.

Thankfully, they sink at once instead of bobbing along with us. Steffi takes one of the shallow bowls we managed to pack and scoops sea water into the canoe. We scrub the inside with grass to get rid of the smell. The seawater does its magic. By the time we're done, the smell of charred flesh has dissipated.

Steffi and I move back into our old canoe with our old treasures in their now charred box. Even though I'm still a little queasy, it feels good to be back in it. It feels right. The others spread out over the three rafts.

We paddle on, exhausted but determined. Steffi looks ready to cry, but she doesn't. I'm too worn out to cry. And if I did, it wouldn't be for those kids. It would be for myself. And my inability to care anymore.

TERROR NUMBER THREE

I watch it approach in the telescope. A small island with a rocky mountain in the center. I don't spot any kids. Or slugs. Or much else. An uninhabitable lump of rock, not a tree or blade of grass.

"Should we bother stopping?" Steffi says. She can't see the island yet, but I describe it to her.

We take out the map and unroll it. We left the map of Anansi Island behind, but the map we found on Mukade Island shows not only that island, but the ones after it. Now that we've rolled the slightly charred scroll out, we notice something else.

"Mukade Island," Steffi says. "It's gone."

"It's scrolled right off the map," I say. "Look. I see a new one behind the island we're heading to."

"Cool," Frank says, swimming up to our canoe. "How do you think that happened?"

Nadia bobs next to him. "It's magic."

Steffi nods. "Or something like it. The map on Anansi Island worked the same way. It changed when anything new happened. When Spike made safe zones of some tunnels, they showed up on the map. Whenever Goliath chewed out a new tunnel, it showed up too."

"So why bother stopping at the next island, if nobody's on it?" Frank asks. "Why don't we keep going?"

"That island might have a treasure on it," Steffi says.

"Exactly," I say. "See the mountain here? Right in the center. See the black dot, close to the top? That's a cave entrance, I'll bet you anything. We should check out that cave before we go any further."

Nadia shakes her head. "I don't want to go in there," she splutters. "What if something bad lives in it?"

"And with no kids around to tell us what that bad thing might be," Frank puts in, "we'll have no idea what we're getting ourselves in to."

"We have Spike," I say, "and he can help us out."

Steffi nods. "You guys can stay on the beach and guard the boats, if you want," she says, "but Jack and I are going up that mountain. We've got a job to do."

"I don't see why it matters," Rob says.

Steffi turns to him. "It *does* matter."

I nod. "It's part of the game, Rob. It's like a weird treasure hunt in a way; we're collecting things. The knife, telescope, and map from Mukade Island and the axe from Anansi Island. We need those things on our journey. The telescope and map help us navigate, and the weapons...well..."

Rob frowns. "Well, what?"

"I think Steffi's right. We'll need them further on. For some kind of fight. And there's something on this island too that we'll need later on. If we don't find it, we'll never solve the puzzle that gets us out of here and back home."

Rob rubs his nose. "You've given this a lot of thought, I guess, but how do you know? Is it just a feeling again?"

"Yes, Rob. Feelings have gotten us this far. I have to trust them."

We fall silent. I stare ahead through the telescope. "How long do you think before we'll reach it?" Keiko asks, steering her raft a bit closer to our canoe.

"Another day maybe. It isn't as far as Anansi Island was from Mukade Island."

Steffi squints. "I think I can see it. Over... there."

I lower the telescope. A small gray smudge breaks the horizon. "Yup, that's it."

I put away the telescope and lay back in the canoe. We can't do anything but wait for the current to take us there. I glance at the map again.

"You realize all these islands are pretty much in a straight line?" I say. "Isn't that weird? And the current must go past all of them."

"I wonder if there's another current that could take us back the way we came," Frank says.

I study the map. It shows the islands and their topography but doesn't annotate anything in the sea.

"What do you think we'll find when we get there?" Steffi says.

I shrug. "Another box, I guess."

"And then?"

"If nobody lives on that island, and I don't think anybody does, we head out to the next one." I point to the map. A long island lined with craggy peaks lies past the lone mountain we're heading for. That island is larger than any we have visited so far, including Mukade Island. "There's bound to be kids living there. Look how big it is."

"Still," Steffi says, lowering her voice, "there's gotta be something menacing about the island we're approaching. Whether any kids live there or not. If there's treasure on it, you can bet something guards it."

I nod. "I'm sure something does. But don't go freaking the others out. Let's get there first and find out what we need to do."

<<<>>>

By mid-afternoon, the mountain looms in front of us, purple in the pink light. We're still some ways off shore, and at the rate we're going we won't land until after the lights click off, which unnerves me. Dark is always when the creepy crawlies come out, and unless they're mukade, we won't know how to handle them.

"Can we get out of this current?" Frank says. "If we could slow down, we could spend the night in the boats and land in the morning."

We take up oars and row parallel to the shore. After a half hour steady paddling, the boats slow down. "I think we're out of it," Steffi says. "Keep rowing."

Nadia squints, staring over her raft's bow. "I see another island!"

"It must be the island behind this one," Steffi says.

"No," I say, staring at the hazy line on the horizon. "That'd be the other direction."

"Maybe there's an island this way too," Steve says.

I check the map. "Just Anansi Island. That's the way we came."

"It's not the lightning cloud again is it?" Nadia whimpers.

"No," Steffi says, gripping the side of the canoe. "It's something else."

The line grows bigger. And bigger. It's rushing right towards us. I peer through the telescope and drop it immediately.

"Oh my God," I whisper. "It's a wave."

Steffi gulps, sinking down until only her eyes peer over the boat. "A wave?"

"A tsunami. It's coming this way."

The wave is heading right for the island. Huge and towering, it covers the sky as it approaches. No sound, no roar, just a silent moving mass of water. It hasn't crested yet.

"Row towards it," I say, grabbing my oar.

"What, are you mad?" Steffi asks. She's shaking on the canoe's floor, curled now in a fetal position. She can't even look at it.

"We can't row *away* from it. The closer we get to the island, the higher that wave is going to get, and it's eventually going to crest. We have to ride *over* it. It's the only way."

We're still far enough from the island that it might be possible. The wave, which way out to sea was probably no more than a ripple, is getting close to land, slowing down, and rising under the pressure. It won't be long before that monster slams down and pummels forward, devouring everything in its path.

The kids in the other rafts grab their oars and paddle towards the rising wave. I desperately shove my oar into the water, pushing forward. The canoe is too big to move on my own. "C'mon!" I yell at Steffi. "We need to reach that wave before it breaks."

She peeks up, takes one look at the oncoming wall of water, and faints.

Spike flutters along the bow, shrieking, then gets smart and flies high into the air, well above the tsunami's reach. He'll be okay. The other kids' rafts are yards ahead already, plowing through the water with everyone who can grab an oar rowing, in a desperate attempt to reach the wave's summit before it crashes down. I paddle as hard as I can, but can't handle both oars. Steffi's body lies limp on the canoe floor.

The other rafts rise as the wave picks them up. They shoot up the wave, the water vaulting them to the sky.

I drop my oar and grab the canoe's side, praying I've rowed enough to make it. The ride up is terrifying. A huge sheet of orange water blocks out the sky. An eternity later, a sliver of pink stabs my eyes, and I shut them tight as we plunge down to meet the sea, meters below. It's the most petrifying, exhilarating roller coaster ride ever: petrifying because I don't know what's going to happen when we reach the bottom but exhilarating because we're on the wave's other side and hopefully through the worst of it.

As the wave speeds away and I realize we aren't going to end up at the bottom of the sea, I turn and watch its progress. It slams into the island, rushing up the mountain's bare sides before churning back towards us, a rush of boiling water that propels us backwards. I grip the sides and ride it out.

"Now we know why that island is so barren," Frank yells, rowing his raft closer to the canoe. "Where's Steffi?"

I point my oar at Steffi, who is still out cold. "Fainted."

Sarah laughs. "We've apparently found Superwoman Steffi's weakness. She's scared of big waves."

"What if there's another wave out there?" Nadia asks. "Sometimes, with tsunamis, there's more than one. There might be an even bigger wave coming."

I shake my head. "I don't think so, Nadia. That wave isn't like a normal tsunami. It's sent on purpose."

"You think?" she breathes, watching the swirling water around us.

"I *know*. It's like the lightning cloud and the things that devour Mukade Island. Each island has its own terror, remember? The wave is this island's terror. Maybe kids did live on this island once. But unless they can escape up to that cave where the wave can't reach, they'd perish, wouldn't they?"

"The wave must come often," Frank says. "That island is completely barren. If it had time to recuperate, trees, or at least grass, would grow on it. The wave keeps it clean."

"How often, do you think?" Bhasker asks, gazing behind us.

Frank shrugs. "Probably every couple of weeks, like the lightning cloud."

I stare at the sea. "I don't think it will come again, not for a while anyway. Not until we leave, I hope."

The island gets smaller. The back eddy of the wave is drawing us away. "We'd better row back out of the current," I say.

I alternately paddle and splash seawater on Steffi. She sits up, spluttering. "What happened?" she whispered.

151

"Tsunami. Don't you remember?"

"Oh God," she moans, sitting up shakily. "I thought I dreamt that."

"You fainted," Sarah yells from her raft.

"Did I? How embarrassing. It was just too real."

"Of course it was, but nobody else fainted," Sarah says.

"Boy, do I feel stupid," Steffi says. "But man, the thought of tsunamis always terrified me. If I have nightmares they're never about spiders or ghosts, they're about huge waves sweeping me away. I'm sure that has some meaning. I never expected to meet up with a real one. I'm sorry."

"So the unshakable Steffi does have something she's scared of," I say, forgiving her. She couldn't help it. "Well, now that you're up, help me row. We have to get back out of the current."

The lights have clicked off before we finally feel that we're in a safe spot. "We should keep rowing and get to land," Steffi says. "What if that tsunami comes back at night?"

"It's probably safer out here than it is on that island," I say, yawning. "That's too steep a mountain to scale in the dark. We'd be sitting ducks on the beach. Let's get some sleep, if we can. We'll deal with that island tomorrow."

<<<>>>

"Wake up!" Steffi hisses in my ear. "It's early morning, doesn't look like there's a creeping critter anywhere out there, and it's time for us to land."

I reach over the canoe's side and grab a few handfuls of water for breakfast. "Let's go."

We land on the rocky shore and drag the boats up the beach. I can see how far up the mountain the wave reached. We need to haul the boats past that point. Just in case.

The entire island is made up of rock. Rocky beach. Rocky mountain. The steep sides are slippery with crumbly stones that slide out from under our feet. Hauling the boats out of danger's way is a struggle. By the time we get them past the water line, we need to go back down for a drink.

"There isn't any fresh water anywhere, it looks like," Steffi says as we wash ourselves off and take gulps of the still turbid seawater. It isn't very clear, it is still full of rocks and dust, but we slurp through it anyway.

We start up the mountain. Whatever secrets it holds, they're buried deep within. And we must find them. Before we can move on.

BUTTERFLY ISLAND

"Send Spike in first," Steffi says.

We stand grouped around the cave entrance. Far below us the orange sea stretches to the horizon. Nadia, Rafael, and Zane cling to the cliff face, staring down the crumbly path we just climbed. Without any trees or bushes to break the view, even to me the height is terrifying. Adrenaline got us up here. I'm not sure what will get us back down that steep slope.

Spike chirps and flitters around the opening. Well, he *is* a bat. He's primed for this sort of thing. We don't have any lights, which means once we're in that tunnel only I will see the hazy outlines of rock, ceiling, floor. Anyone who braves it with me will have to blindly follow.

We huddle against the cliff face and wait for Spike to finish his exploring.

"Look at that view," Steffi says. "You can almost see Anansi Island from here."

Spike flies out of the dark.

"He says there's nothing down there except the box," I say. "And a huge, shriveled-up butterfly. It's been dead for a while."

"I wonder if that's this island's evil," Rob says.

"And if it's the only one," Frank adds.

154

I shrug. "If there were other butterflies here, what would they eat? This island is dead. Spike didn't see any traces of mukade, spiders, slugs, kids, anything."

"*Why* is the island dead?" Frank murmurs. "That's what I want to know."

"Look, we all don't have to go down there," I say. "Steve and I can grab the box and get it back up here. The rest of you can stay here." I glance at Steffi, who has already started fuming.

"Why do you want *me* to stay? Since I fainted on the boat, now I'm a wuss?"

"Steve doesn't have his arm in a cast."

Steffi flexes her arm. "It's been getting stronger every day," she says, scowling. "I'm perfectly capable of lugging a box back up."

I know better than to argue with her. She'll probably just follow us in anyway. "Fine. Let's go."

We inch down the crumbing slope, Steve following me and Steffi taking up the rear. Steve's hand grips my shoulder like a vise. "Don't worry, I'm won't lose you," I say. "Ease up, I don't need a broken collar bone before we leave here."

The steep passage descends into the heart of the mountain. After fifteen minutes of steady descent, we enter a vast cavern. A small trickle of water flows through a gully and we stop for a drink. The water is cold and sweet.

"This is the one water source the island has, I bet," I say, my voice echoing through the still, silent room. "If kids did live here, they'd have to climb down here whenever they were thirsty."

"Do you see the butterfly?" Steve whispers.

"Yeah. It's curled over there, next to the box. It must've been guarding it when it died."

"You sure it's dead?"

"Steve, it's half decomposed and is missing a wing. Unless it has the ability to rejuvenate itself, it isn't coming after us."

I make light of it, but I'm glad they can't see the butterfly. It's huge and deathly white, like any color it might have had has faded away. It looks so much like an evil ghost that I'm happy to get away from it. For a fleeting moment, I wonder what would happen if a monster bug like that ever met up with Pooky. That would be a fight worth watching.

The box isn't too heavy, but trudging back up the slope exhausts me. We take turns carrying the box, and even so the fifteen minute descent down turns into a good half hour ascent back. By the time we reach the fresh outside air, night has fallen. Sarah is waiting for us, shivering on the ledge.

"It's freezing out here," she says. "What took you so long? We were getting worried."

"It's okay," I say. "We found the box. Where's everyone else?"

"I sent 'em down before the lights clicked off. There's grass in the boats. That's all the blanket we've got; we should get down there before we all come down with hypothermia."

I'm warm, sweating even, but I know that after my body cools down from the exercise, I'll be freezing too. There's nothing colder than sitting around in sweaty clothes, and I don't have anything else to change into. The clothes clinging to my skin are the same ones I first came to this place in. The pants are getting too tight, but they'll last a little longer. Steffi's in the same boat as me. Her jeans are in shreds. She walks with bare feet. My left sneaker now has a hole in it, and it won't be long before I'll have to ditch the shoes and harden my soles like Steffi has. She can walk on sharp glass and not feel it.

We store the box in the canoe and climb into the rafts with the others. We all huddle under the grass, lying side-by-side for warmth. Steffi wiggles close to me on one side. She shivers, but warmth still radiates from her body. I put my arms around her. She snuggles up to my chest and sighs. Her shivering stops and her breathing becomes slow, deep. She is asleep.

As tired as I am, it takes a lot longer for me to enter the same zone.

<<<>>>

"So what's in the box?" Sarah says, shaking me awake. "Let's open it up, the suspense has been killing me all night."

I blink. "Maybe we should get some breakfast first."

"No, c'mon. Open the box."

We use the knife and axe to pry the box open. Steffi digs in and pulls out a glittering rattle covered in sparkling stones.

"Wow," Zane says, grabbing it out of Steffi's hands and giving it a shake.

Steffi grins. "Whatever baby gets that thing would be spoiled for life. You think those are diamonds?"

"That isn't meant for a baby," I say. "I bet it's to scare off the butterfly."

"You think?" Frank asks, peering at it.

"Yeah, it's like how the shield on Anansi Island controls Pooky. I'll bet that's what it's for, anyway."

Steffi digs deeper. "There's gotta be a weapon in here," she says, "if the box stays true to form." She pulls out a small blunt object with four holes in it. Red stones cover the object.

Steve peers at it. "That look like brass knuckles," he says.

Steffi slips the rings over her fingers. She clenches her hand into a fist and pounds the ground.

"Anything else?" I say.

"Well, there's a map, of course," she says, pulling out the now-familiar roll. "And...what's this?"

She reaches in and hefts out a bronze bowl. The words "DRINK ME" have been stamped into the rim.

"That reminds me of something," Steffi says, running a finger over the words, "but I can't remember what."

Zane pokes his face close to the bowl. "There's nothing in it," he says. "What are we supposed to drink?"

"Dunno," Steffi says, "but I suppose it has something to do with how this island works. Or worked, back when there was life on it."

We consolidate our other treasures to the new box and discard the charred one. Nadia takes the rattle from Zane and rolls it around in her hand. "Do you think we should leave this here? In case any kid shows up and has to use it?"

"Against what?" Steffi says. "The butterfly is dead; Jack saw it."

"They could always put a new one here," I say.

Sarah frowns. "They? Who do you think *they* is?"

I shrug. "I dunno, Sarah. But someone has laid out this whole game."

"I vote we take it with us," Nadia says. "It looks valuable. Maybe if we ever get back home, we can sell it."

I shrug again. It doesn't make much difference. If somebody can put another butterfly here, they can always throw in another rattle.

There's nothing else to do on this dead island, so we drag the boats towards the shore. Halfway there, Frank, Zane, and Terry, who are dragging the raft, stop.

"The tide's going out," Frank says, turning around. "Fast. Get back up the mountain!"

"What is it?" Steffi asks.

"Another wave's coming. We aren't above the waterline. Move!"

We haul the boats back up to their resting place and turn around in time to see a huge wave spanning into the sky. A hundred feet, at least. It curls over and pounces, crashing down and rolling forward, careening up the mountain's slope in a thunderous roar. I drop the canoe and run.

The others follow. I can't even think about the canoe. Trying to save it doesn't matter compared to saving my own skin. The ground begins to shake, and we scramble frantically along the crumbling trail. I reach the cavern ledge and stop, turning around.

The wave is already retreating. It didn't reach the boats. I sink to the ground, gasping. Steffi claws her way up next to me.

"That was close," she says after she gets her breath back. "Did everyone make it?"

I stare down the slope. Not everyone has made it up to the ledge, but it looks like the tsunami didn't claim any victims.

"The wave must come every day," Frank says.

"It happened right before the lights clicked off, the night before last," I say. "So every other day, at least. No wonder nothing lives here."

We watch as the wave recedes and the boiling sea calms. It's a good while before we get the courage to leave the ledge and descend to the boats.

"Figure we have a couple of days to get well away from this island before that wave comes again," Steffi says. "I hope that current is still there, and it's strong enough to pull us out to sea quick."

I nod, staring at the ground as we inch down the crumbly mountain.

Spike lands on my shoulder and chirps into my ear. I stop. Steffi careens into me from behind, almost toppling me down the mountain.

"Watch it!" she says. "Don't stop like that without giving me a warning."

"Steffi," I say, "Spike says there's another kid here."

"Where?" She whips her head around. "We haven't seen anybody this whole time."

"No," I say. "The kid just got here."

"You mean, like through a portal?"

I nod. "He's in the cave's mouth. What do we do?"

"What do you mean, 'what do we do?' We wake him up."

"And then what?" I shake my head, hating myself for thinking this way. The thought screams through my head: *we can't take this kid with us. He'll never make it.* But if we leave him here, the poor kid will starve to death. Or the tsunami will wash him away.

"God," Steffi whispers. "How horrible. Do you think kids pop up here regularly? Can you imagine? Even without worrying about the butterfly, you're doomed. There's nothing here to eat."

"We'll have to take him with us," Frank says.

"How? He'll burn up in the sea. He can't drink the seawater. He'd die of thirst out there."

My stomach begins to lurch. The thought keeps flitting through my mind: *get out of here now. Leave. Before you set eyes on that poor kid and feel the need to save him.*

Steffi is already pushing back up the mountain. It's too late. She isn't going to leave without doing something about that kid.

I fight down my nausea and follow.

THE OTHER SIDE

A skinny boy with dirty blond hair lies in the cave's mouth, and I wonder how often that butterfly crouched here, waiting. How many kids ever even woke up after they arrived? Not many, I'd bet. It'd be hard to escape down that cliff, with a monster that could fly after you. Even if they did wake up, if they managed to escape the insect, where would they go? What would they eat? This kid, if we weren't here to find him, wouldn't last more than a day or two. He won't last long even with us, and we'll have to watch him suffer as he dies. I tell this to Steffi.

"Not necessarily, she says, sitting down next to the still comatose boy. "We can catch fish for him. He can eat that."

"We'll have to brave the tsunami whenever we need to get him food," I say. "That wave isn't predictable. You never know when it's going to show up."

"We'll have to brave it when we want to drink the seawater too, Jack. Look, we don't have a perfect situation here, but what other choice is there? We can't let the poor kid wake up and die here, can we?"

We can. I don't say it because I know it's wrong. I'm still hating myself for even sticking this idea in the viable option category. Now that I've seen the boy, all small and innocent

161

lying on the ground, of course I can't abandon him. When he was faceless, I might have. I would have regretted it my whole life maybe, but I could have walked away.

"We can't take him with us," I say. "That's for certain."

Steve bites his lip. "Jack, if what you think is true, and this whole world is laid out like some sort of game, then this island must work like the others, right? There must be a secret hidden on it somewhere...a way to immunize him."

I frown. "It could take days to figure that out, though."

"I bet it doesn't take too long. We know now that there's a trick to all these islands. There's always a protector—the mukade on our island, Pooky on Anansi Island, and here it was the butterfly, we're guessing. There's always a way to control the protector too. Here it's the rattle...again, we're guessing. So there must be a way to immunize the kids here. Like the mukade bites and the potion on Mukade Island. And the blue dots in that pond on Anansi Island."

"But there's nothing here," Steffi says.

"There's gotta be. Let's take a closer look at the map."

Steffi pulls the map out of the box. We study it.

"We're on this side," Steve says, "but look at the other side. Doesn't that look like a lagoon?"

I nod. "Maybe it's sheltered there. From the wave."

Steffi stands. "We should go check it out. Not all of us have to go. Jack?"

I nod. "We'll take the canoe. We should be able to pull it right into that lagoon."

The kid stirs. Steffi shakes him. Not in the frantic way she shook me awake when she first found me, lying in that corridor on Mukade Island. No, we have nothing to run from here. The kid can take his time waking up and getting his bearings.

He manages to say his name: Sven. From Sweden, I think. He knows a little English but it's garbled. He is in shock. I wonder what he wished for, when he was given the opportunity. He gazes blankly at us, then points to his throat.

"Water," he whispers.

"Yeah, you gotta be thirsty after that," I say, remembering how parched I felt when I first woke up.

Frank and I clamber back down to the stream and fill a bowl. "This is going to be a pain," I say. "All we have are these bowls, and we only have two. The rest of us can drink the seawater, but that kid'll probably go through ten of these a day."

We climb out of the mountain. Steffi is waiting, so restless she's almost tap dancing on the rocks. The kid slurps down practically all the water.

"How long do you think it'll take us to get to the other side of the island and back?" Steffi whispers. "He's gonna be thirsty soon, and you're the only one who can see clearly enough to get down to that stream."

"Maybe I should stay and someone else should go with you," I say.

She grabs my hand. "No. It's you and me, Jack. We braved the mukade, we found the pond, and we have to do this together, too."

"Let's go then," I say.

We leave the others and lug the canoe to the waterline. Steffi looks scared—I bet she's wondering if that tsunami might play a trick and visit us early—but she braves it, and we begin paddling.

"Jack," she says. "Thanks."

"For what?"

"For staying and helping that kid. I know you didn't want to."

She knows me so well it's almost scary. "You're welcome" would sound weird to say, so I don't say anything. I don't need to.

We row in silence. Calm waves lap on the shore. As we glide along the coast and round the other side, the look of the island begins to change.

"Wow," Steffi says. "I guess the tsunami can't get to this side, can it?"

I nod, speechless. Where ugly rock had covered one side of the island, this side grows more and more lush. By the time we reach the opposite side, huge green ferns and bright red and yellow flowers blanket the rocks. Tall, wavering palms line a white sand beach. A waterfall rumbles down the mountain and spills into a bright pink lagoon.

"This is paradise," Steffi whispers.

"Yeah," I say, steering toward the lagoon, "you think that now. But can you imagine, sitting on this beach, waiting for that butterfly to zoom over the trees, dive down, and grab you for lunch?"

"I wonder why the butterfly died," Steffi says. "And why there aren't any kids here."

"There's fruit," I say. "And coconuts. And fresh water. Kids wouldn't go hungry here, that's for sure."

We wade through the shallow water, pull the canoe onto the white beach, and gaze around. "I suppose if we had to leave Sven here, he'd do okay," I say.

Steffi frowns. "Yeah, but if what you say is true, we should be able to make him immune to the seawater and he can come with us."

I sigh. "By the time we pass all these islands, we'll have a whole *flotilla* of kids."

"Maybe that's part of the game," Steffi says. "Maybe you have to collect kids from all the islands."

"Yeah, but I don't get why I have such a...desire...to leave without them. All of them, except you, Steffi. I feel so...horrible in a way. Like I'm willing to leave their fates up to chance, just so I can go on without them."

She frowns and scrutinizes the beach. "I feel that too. I didn't really before. But now that feeling is strong...that we should go on alone."

164

"It's funny. I didn't feel this way when we left Mukade Island," I say. "I wanted to save The Others and take them with us, remember?"

"I remember. But they were trying to kill us. What choice did we have?"

I frown, remembering my first thought when Spike told me about Sven. *Don't go back. Leave him here.* We had faced the same choice on Mukade Island as I had here. There, Steffi goaded us forward and I thought she was horrible, not going back to rescue those kids. Here, I was about to do the same.

"Anyway," Steffi says, "how can we make Sven immune to the seawater?"

I plop down on the white sand. "Immunity on Mukade Island had to do with the mukade themselves. But immunity on Anansi Island had nothing to do with the spider. It had to do with what the spider was guarding. The pond. So maybe there's something the butterfly was guarding. Maybe it's inside the mountain."

We turn our heads away from the water. Above us, the tip of the rocky mountain pokes over the foliage. A dark spot appears above the tree line...a cave.

"There must be a path up there from here," Steffi says.

I get up. "Let's go, then."

We clamber up a steep, rocky path. Steffi keeps her knife ready in case, but we don't meet up with any nasty creatures or poisonous plants. Just trees laden with fruit and the beautiful, sweet-smelling flowers.

"You know, it seems like every island gets easier to maneuver," Steffi says as we climb. "Mukade Island had all sorts of traps...the sharp grass, the mukade, the snakes on The Others' side...but all Anansi Island had was Pooky. And this place...doesn't seem to have anything. Any more."

"Don't jinx it," I say, watching Spike flutter ahead of us. He doesn't seem concerned or agitated.

We pull ourselves up to the entrance. Spike grabs my hair, and we step into the cool darkness of the cave. I stare around and gasp.

"What?" Steffi says, gripping my shoulder. "What is it?"

"Mushrooms," I say.

"What?"

The entire floor of this room is covered with massive mushrooms. White, with huge, bright spots of different colors. Spike chirps.

"They're growing in a pile of poo," I say.

Steffi stumbles a bit. "Butterfly poo? *Do* butterflies poo?"

"I don't know. It doesn't smell, anyway."

"Mushrooms," Steffi says. "Like Alice in Wonderland."

"What?"

"It's an old book my mum gave me to read once. Really strange, but this girl Alice ate a mushroom to grow taller. Or shrink. I can't remember which. Hey! I've got it. 'Drink Me'."

I'm not following her train of thought at all. "What?"

"That was part of Alice in Wonderland too, and it was stamped on the bowl we found. Jack, I'll be anything these mushrooms are how Sven can get immune to the seawater."

I touch one of the mushroom caps. It's soft like velvet. "How do you figure?"

"Well, the box always contains things we need to solve the island's mysteries, right? The bowl has to be for something, I bet we're supposed to use it to mix up some kind of mushroom concoction."

"Seems pretty easy," I say.

"Exactly. Every island gets easier. Let's collect some of these mushrooms and bring them back with us. I bet Keiko can figure out how to make a good brew."

We gather the mushrooms and clamber back to the canoe.

"If the butterfly is dead," Steffi says as we push off, "there won't be any more of these mushrooms for new kids."

"Maybe there *won't* be any new kids," I say.

She turns to me. "What do you mean?"

"Well, it's like you said about these islands getting easier to figure out. Maybe the closer we get to the end of this game the less new kids show up. I mean, we were on Anansi Island for more than two weeks and not a single new kid showed up in that time."

"I wonder why Sven showed up then," Steffi says. "Right when we were about to leave."

I shrug. "Maybe part of the game is that we have to find out all the island's secrets. How to get immune is part of that. Without Sven showing up, we wouldn't have bothered."

"Why would that be important though?" Steffi says.

Spike chirps softly near my ear. I smile. "Because it's the only way to go forward," I say. "Once we completely figure out the puzzle, we're allowed to move on."

Steffi frowns. "I wonder what would have stopped us if we *hadn't* searched for the immunity factor."

I shrug. "We had to search for it. They sent Sven to make sure of it."

"'They' again." Steffi stares into the magenta sky. "I wonder if 'they' are watching us right now."

It works. After we move everyone to the lagoon side of the island, Steve starts a fire and Keiko boils up a brew with the mushrooms. We hold our breath as Sven drinks it, but it isn't long before he is splashing in the lagoon with the other kids.

As I watch them, Frank comes over and sits in the sand next to me.

"This place is much nicer than Anansi Island," he says. "By a long shot."

"It's a bit weird, don't you think?" Sarah says, plopping down next to Frank. "Why would the tsunami only hit the other side? It doesn't seem like much of a hard thing to avoid. Stay away from that side, and you're golden."

Steffi sits cross-legged in front of us, her back to the lagoon. "Yeah, it's easier. This tsunami isn't so bad...I mean, if you can avoid it," she says, reddening. "The lightning on Anansi Island was worse, but not as bad as the things that ate up everything on Mukade Island. The farther we sail, the easier things get."

"So maybe..." Rob says, throwing himself down in the sand, "...the next island will be even nicer."

"Or there aren't any more," Sarah says. "Maybe if we keep sailing, we'll find the way out."

I shake my head. "No. There's more."

"How do you know?"

"Well, the map for one. It shows an island past this one. And for another..."

I pause. Steffi reaches over and squeezes my arm.

Sarah frowns. "For another what?"

"I'm looking for someone," I say. "Don't ask me who or why. All I know is there's somebody here that I need to find...someone that'll show us how to get out of here. How to end this."

Sarah sighs and stares out at the placid lagoon and laughing kids. "And you don't need us for that, do you?"

"No," I say. "I don't."

Frank clears his throat. "I think you all should stay here. Jack and Steffi are right...the only thing you have to worry about here is the tsunami, and only if you're dumb enough to venture to the other side."

Nadia, whose limp lessens a bit every time she swims in the seawater, jogs, dripping, up to us and frowns. "What do you mean 'you'?"

"You're not thinking of coming with Jack and me, are you?" Steffi says.

Frank clears his throat. "No. I want to go find my brother. I want to sail to Mukade Island."

Sarah shakes her head. "Not a good idea."

"Besides, how would you do it?" I say.

'Well, there seems to be two currents...one that pulls you forward and one that can take you back. This morning, after we had breakfast, Terry and I took a raft and floated around the other side. We got caught in a current that pulled us the opposite way. We had to row hard to get out of it. We circled the whole island to get into the right current that would take us back here. I think that opposite current flows past Anansi Island. And past that, Mukade Island." He licks his lips. "My brother is there. I want to go back and get him."

Sarah shudders. "I don't want those kids coming here."

"I can convince him to be good," Frank says. "I know I can. We can't leave them there to die. Not now that we know this place exists."

As much as I hated Mike Mullens, I understand why Frank wants so badly to find him. I want to find my brother, too. It's not my place to tell Frank what to do, any more than it is for him to tell me.

And maybe on the next island I'll get lucky. Maybe my brother Cody will be there, waiting for me.

<<<>>>

Frank, Steffi, and I decide to begin our journeys after the next tsunami hits. Early in the morning we hear it crashing against the far shore. The ground rumbles, and we watch the now split wave roar past our beach and vanish to the left and right. We never even get a ripple in the lagoon.

Before it fully vanishes, Frank has his raft in the water. He's going solo: the other kids from Anansi Island want to stay here. So do I, to be honest. There's something peaceful and secure about this place, like nothing can harm us in this pink lagoon. It's the first time I've felt this sort of safety since the real world blinked out of existence.

But we're leaving too, Steffi and I. Steve, Sarah, Bhasker, Rob, and Keiko have opted to stay on Butterfly Island, as we've now named it. Steve seemed almost sheepish when he told us, as if he felt like he was letting us down. But he isn't. Everything is falling into place now. *This* island is the ultimate Safe Zone. This is where everyone is meant to stay. This is where Steffi and I head out alone, like we always planned.

"We should go," Steffi says. "Before we get too used to this place.

We hug the others goodbye and push the canoe into the lagoon. "I feel bad," Steffi says to Steve. "If Frank takes one raft, and we take the canoe, you don't have enough rafts for everyone, if you need to leave the island."

Steve laughs. "Look around, Steffi. There's plenty of wood here. I know how to build a boat. I will, when the time comes."

"What do you mean?" Steffi says.

He smiles, hugs her, and gives me a slap on the back. "I think there'll be a time when we'll know we should hit the sea and follow you. It isn't now, though. But it'll happen, I feel it. When Jack finds who he's looking for and figures out how to get home...I think right about then I'll get a big urge to chop down a few trees and start building."

I raise my eyebrows. "You really think so?"

He grins. "You're not the only one who can have premonitions. Bye, Jack."

I shake his hand. "Bye, Steve. Bye, Bhasker. Sarah."

Sarah grips me in a bear hug. She even hugs Steffi. "Bye guys. We'll be okay here. Don't worry about us."

"But you'll come back for us, right?" Rob says, now looking a bit panicked at the thought of us leaving. He sounds so sad. Steffi turns to him. She smiles, then puts her arms around him and gives him a squeeze.

"We'll be back," she says. "I promise." She turns to Keiko, and they hug. "Take care of anyone else who shows up on this island."

"Got it," Keiko whispers. They break apart. Rob looks at me.

"Find what you need to find," he says, "and then come back. Please. Don't forget us."

"I won't," I say, and this time I'm sure of it. "I promise."

Steffi pushes the canoe into the water. We jump in and head for the current. I glance back. Smiling kids wave to us from the beach. On the island's far side, I spot Frank, steadily rowing in the opposite direction.

I hope he finds a current. As much as I loathe Mike Mullens, I hope Frank can reunite with his brother.

I watch him until the current sucks his boat around Butterfly Island and the mountain blocks my view. Whatever happens to him now, it's out of our hands.

I glance back at Steffi. The soft breeze rustles her red hair, and her eyes stare out at the vast orange sea ahead of us. I wonder if she's thinking the same thing I am. What new adventure lies out there, waiting for us? Will we find the stranger we so desperately seek? If we find him, will he show us how to get out of this place and back home?

I lean back, take Steffi's hand and squeeze it. Her fingers squeeze back. At least we're together. Whatever lies out there, we'll face it head-on. The two of us.

Butterfly Island is already vanishing in a misty haze. I turn my gaze forward and take a deep breath. I don't look back again.

ABOUT THE AUTHOR

Originally from Virginia, Nikki Bennett avidly read C.S. Lewis, J.R.R. Tolkien, and any book that had to do with fantasy while growing up. After spending the first part of her "adult life" on a farm raising horses, she and her husband Steve moved to Japan. There, Nikki developed a love of Asian mythology and history. Nikki now lives in the Pacific Northwes

ANANSI ISLAND is the second book in The Island Chronicles.

Follow Nikki on Patreon!
www.patreon.com/bennettart

OTHER BOOKS BY NIKKI
Mukade Island
Moka Island
From the Magical Mind of Mindy Munson
Four Fiends
Three Treasures
The Trouble with Dead People
9th Street Ninjas

Keep reading for a sneak peek of the next book in the series!

THE GAME

There it is. I can see it."

"What does it look like, Jack?"

"Huge. Lots of craggy mountains. Smoke."

"Smoke?"

Steffi sits up and turns her head in the direction of my telescope but she can't see anything. We're too far away. Our canoe bobs along on a quiet orange sea, no land in sight. If I weren't gazing through the telescope, I wouldn't see anything either. But with the telescope the island is perfectly clear. A desolate landscape hugs the skyline. I can't tell how tall the mountains are; they get lost in the low cloud of smoke.

"Volcanoes, do you think?" Steffi says.

"I don't know. I see a gravelly beach where we can land, at least. But man...those mountains go on forever."

She sighs. "No pretty palm trees or pink lagoons like the last island, I guess."

"Not that I can see. But maybe they're all hiding on the other side of the island."

Steffi leans back in the canoe and trails her arm in the warm water. "I wonder if it's dead, like the last island was."

Butterfly Island. It wasn't totally dead. One side of the island was full of trees and flowers. But nothing lived on it. We left the other kids there three days ago, except for Frank, who launched his raft in the opposite current and headed for Mukade Island.

"I wonder if we'll see any of them again," I mutter.

Steffi doesn't respond. I put the telescope away and face her. With only two of us in it, the canoe has lots of space and we both stretch out. She faces the direction of Butterfly Island and I stare at the new island. We have a couple of days to go before we get there, I'm guessing, depending on if the current we're in picks up pace or slows down.

"Well," she says. "We'd better plan a strategy. One: land. Two: find the box. Three: if there are any kids on that island, figure out how to immunize 'em against whatever evil this island throws at us."

"Even if there aren't any kids, we'll have to figure out the immunity trick," I say. "It's part of the game."

"What if we don't? What if we just skip this island completely and keep going? How do you know this 'game' theory of yours is correct?"

I shrug. "I don't. But that seems to be how it's worked so far."

Steffi chews a fingernail thoughtfully. "You know, there was one weird thing about the last island. There was no good guy on it."

"Come again?"

She leans forward, reaches out, and scratches Spike's belly. The little purple bat hangs off an outrigger pole, snoozing. He doesn't usually sleep much, but even he is getting bored with staring at nothing but flat orange sea.

"Mukade Island had the bats, like Spike," she says. "They helped us when we needed it. Anansi Island had Goliath, the big worm. He did the same thing. But Butterfly Island didn't have a helper. We found the dead butterfly...that was the island's evil...but we never found the good guy."

"Maybe it was dead, too," I suggest. "Or..." and I don't like to think of this idea much, "...maybe the butterfly was the helper. And the evil...whatever it is...is still lurking around somewhere."

She shudders. "Don't say that. We left all our friends there." She turns her head again, craning to catch a view of the new island. "Jack, if this is a game, and these islands are mapped out the same way, there must've been a helper somewhere on Butterfly Island. And this island coming up...it has to have the same sort of setup, right? An evil that torments the kids. A helper that aids them in figuring out how to escape. And a box that holds the key to solving the island's secrets."

"Don't forget the terror from the sea," I say, remembering the cloud with the black things that ate everything on Mukade Island, the lightning cloud that wreaked havoc on Anansi Island and the tsunami that continually crashed on Butterfly Island.

Steffi shudders. "Exactly. And that's something else. On Mukade Island, the terror came every few years. On Anansi, every couple of weeks, and on Butterfly Island, that tsunami hit every other day. If this new island follows the trend, there's probably some horror every damn afternoon. And we're gonna land right into it without any idea how to survive it."

I hadn't thought too much about this, but leave it to Steffi to ponder these things. I'd been more curious as to what sort of "evil" lived on the approaching island and how we'd protect ourselves from it.

And how, in the multitude of mountainous peaks, we'll find the box with the treasures that will save us.

Steffi reads my thoughts. "It'll be in a cave," she says. "It always is. Somewhere deep underground."

I splash some sea water in my face. "That'll take forever. That island has to be at least twenty miles long, and I'm not sure how wide it is."

"Did you see any kids in that telescope?" she asks.

"No. The beach looked pretty barren."

"Why don't we circle the whole island, then?" she says. "Scout it out first before we land."

"Sounds reasonable, except for the terror from the sea problem," I say. "If we could figure out what that is before we circle the whole island and potentially meet up with it, that would help."

"Mhm." She taps a finger on her cheek, thinking. "You know, the black things that terrorized Mukade Island could only be avoided if you got into the sea. But the lightning cloud on Anansi Island could only be avoided by getting underground, until we got immunity from it. And the only way to avoid the tsunami on Butterfly Island was to stay on the sheltered side, where the pink lagoon was."

"So how do you think we avoid this one?"

She laughs. "No damn clue. But, if the terror comes more frequently than the one on Butterfly Island, we'll find out quick."

She reaches into the treasure box, pulls out the map, and unrolls it. I lean forward and gaze at it. This map is incredibly handy. It shows what's in front of us and what's behind us, and, if we keep sailing, it will eventually show us anything beyond.

The island in front of us is so long it takes up most of the map. Butterfly Island is almost pushed off the bottom of the scroll. And a tiny sliver of a new island is beginning to poke over the top.

"Damn," Steffi says. "There's another island after this one? Does this sea go on forever, or what?"

I feel her frustration. My stomach takes a dive as I stare at the little arm of this new island. I've been hoping the island we're approaching is the last one. The one where I'll find my brother, Cody. And where I'll meet the stranger I've been searching for...the one who can show us how to escape this world, or this hologram, or whatever this reality is...and return home.

Steffi rolls the map up, sighs, and slumps back in her corner of the boat. I do the same. We roll with the current in silence, closer and closer to a place we have no clue about.

Silence. Most of our journey so far has been mired in it. After we had pulled away from the pink lagoon and waved good-bye to our friends, I thought the solitude would bring Steffi and I closer. But an almost depressive silence has filled the boat since we left the others. It's not like we're suddenly scared to talk to each other...that's not it. It feels more like we've sailed into a part of the sea that sucks the energy out of you and makes you want to do nothing but sleep and think and stay silent. This conversation about what lies ahead and how to deal with it has been the most lively talk we've had in two days, but seeing that new island show up on the map...another island...has switched my depressive funk into overdrive.

From his perch, Spike rustles and gives out a sleepy squeak. It's his lazy attempt to let us know the lights are about to click off for the day. Back on Mukade Island, the bats always warned us, loud and shrill, about the approaching night because if we weren't in our cave when the lights went out, we'd become a quick dinner for the giant centipedes that roamed the island at night.

But after we escaped that island and landed on Anansi Island, the need to seek shelter after dark wasn't quite as imperative. The giant spider that roamed that island was active in the day time too, and even though it was easier to spot him when the lights were on, Anansi Island was never completely dark. Even at night it had a luminescent glow to it, enough to see by. And when we reached Butterfly Island, where the evil had already died (if the butterfly was the evil), a light's-out call became totally unnecessary. But, out of habit or some ingrained instinct, Spike still always gave his nightly chirp.

Here on the sea, it doesn't matter at all. There's no difference between night and day. The sea is always flat and still, barely a movement except for the current that pulls us steadily along. The tsunami that crashes into Butterfly Island every other day must peter out quickly once it hits, because we've never even seen a ripple from it.

Whoever created this place didn't give much thought to the sea. They put all their energy into creating horrors for the islands. Once, on our journey away from Mukade Island, we had been attacked by a strange sea monster, but it had disappeared as quickly as it came, and although for a while we'd been on high alert for something like that to happen again, we haven't worried much about it lately. It seems that nothing will happen in this part of the sea. There is no life except Steffi, me, and the snoring bat.

The lights click off. Instantly, the sky switches from bright pink to inky black. In a few minutes, I hear Steffi's light breathing and know she's asleep. I stare at the sky, wishing there were stars to gaze at, but there's nothing up there except black. You can't see anything in the inkiness except through the telescope which has a weird infrared-type of property. I pull it out of the box and stare through it, focusing on the island now covered in darkness.

And I see something new.

Where ten minutes before gentle waves had lapped on the beach, the sea now foams and rolls like someone's put a fire on it and set it to boil. I almost drop the telescope as I watch a long, eely beast burst out of the water and roll back in, followed by another and another until the sea looks like one rolling mass of giant snakes.

I gasp so loud, Steffi wakes. "What? What is it?" she asks, instantly alert, grabbing for the jeweled knife she always keeps strapped to her leg.

I lower the telescope, trying to catch my breath. "Remember that sea monster, Steffi?"

"How could I forget it?" She grips the canoe's edges and turns her head, straining to see what my now telescope-free eye still stares toward. The pitch blackness is suddenly comforting.

"That whole beach is teeming with 'em," I whisper.

"Is there one heading towards us now?" she says.

"No." I steel myself and raise the telescope to my eye. The monsters are now sliding out of the sea and slithering up the rocky shore, heading inland. The beach is so thick with them I can't even see the pebbles.

I move the telescope down the beach, but it's the same everywhere I look. Hundreds...thousands...of huge, snaky monsters flounder out of the water and begin streaming toward the bases of the smoking mountains. There doesn't seem to be a break in the migration anywhere.

"There's no way we can land," I say. "Even in the daytime... those things must live close to shore; we'll never sail through them unnoticed."

"Do you think they'll come into the current?" Steffi whispers.

"What do you mean?"

"This current we're in. It'll loop us right around that island. If they don't come into the current, we could sail past the whole island and try circling it, like we planned. Maybe the other side is monster-free. Maybe we can land there."

"I don't know...that monster we ran into before we got to Anansi Island was in the current. I'm not sure how we'll get through this."

"Well," Steffi says, thinking, "we'll have to stay well away from that island during the day and just float around it at night, when the monsters are all on land. Right?"

I put the telescope down. "That might work."

She scoots down into the boat. "Just makes you wonder though...are those monsters the terror from the sea? Or are they the island's evil?"

I raise the telescope back to my eye. And I see something else.

Hot red lava spurts from the volcanos. The lava flies in the air, but something's odd about it. I zoom in, but it's hard to see through all the smoke.

The lava breaks into small lumps of red that stream upward then float back down around the island, moving to and fro like they're riding some weird air current. They almost looks alive.

"I think," I say, "those monsters are the terror from the sea."

She falls silent, and I study the little blobs of light streaming around the island. The more I watch them, the more I realize they aren't bits of lava after all.

They're living things.

And ten to one, they're the evil we'll have to deal with when we land.

www.ingramcontent.com/pod-product-compliance
Lightning Source LLC
Chambersburg PA
CBHW051512170626
46811CB00002B/782